THE YEAR OF
PERFECT HAPPINESS

STORIES

THE YEAR OF PERFECT HAPPINESS

STORIES

BECKY ADNOT-HAYNES

2014 WINNER, KATHERINE ANNE PORTER PRIZE IN SHORT FICTION

University of North Texas Press
Denton, Texas

10 9 8 7 6 5 4 3 2 1

Permissions:
University of North Texas Press
1155 Union Circle #311336
Denton, Texas 76203-5017

∞The paper used in this book meets the minimum requirements of the American National
Standard for Permanence of Paper for Printed Library Materials, z39.48.1984. Binding
materials have been chosen for durability.

Library of Congress Cataloging-in-Publication Data

Adnot-Haynes, Becky, 1984– author.
[Short stories. Selections]
  The year of perfect happiness : stories / Becky Adnot-Haynes.—First edition.
    pages cm—(Katherine Anne Porter Prize in Short Fiction series ; number 13)
  "2014 Winner, Katherine Anne Porter Prize in Short Fiction."
  ISBN 978-1-57441-565-0 (pbk. : alk. paper)—ISBN 978-1-57441-579-7 (ebook)
  I. Title. II. Series: Katherine Anne Porter Prize in Short Fiction series ; no. 13.
  PS3601.D585A6 2014
  813'.6—dc23
                                    2014026262

The Year of Perfect Happiness is Number 13 in the Katherine Anne Porter Prize in Short
Fiction Series

This is a work of fiction. Any resemblance to actual events or establishments or to persons
living or dead is unintentional.

The electronic edition of this book was made possible by the support of the Vick Family
Foundation.

Cover Art is by Shannon May
Cover and text design by Rose Design

For Kevin, who has given me multiple years of perfect happiness.

Contents

Acknowledgments

Thank you to all of the editors of the publications in which my stories first appeared: "The Year of Perfect Happiness" in *Missouri Review*; "Baby Baby" and "Thank You for the _____" in *Hobart*; "A Natural Progression of Things" in *Post Road*; "Planche, Whip, Salto," in *PANK*; "Grip" in *West Branch*; "Rough Like Wool" in *CutBank*; "The Men" in *Room Magazine*, and "The Second Wife" in *Summerset Review*.

Thank you to Matt Bell for picking my book as the winner of the KAP prize, and thank you to Laura Kopchick and Karen DeVinney for their generous help bringing it into the world.

Thank you to the excellent *Cincinnati Review* crew for their editorial acumen and King-Cake-eating company: Nicola Mason, Matt O'Keefe, Matt McBride, Lisa Ampleman, Brian Trapp, and all of the stellar editorial assistants who I had the happy luck to cross paths with.

An especially big thank-you to my writing teachers and mentors at the University of Cincinnati and Clemson University, who helped me as I figured out what it meant to be a writer: Leah Stewart, Michael Griffith, Brock Clarke, Chris Bachelder, and Keith Morris. You guys rock.

I am deeply indebted to all of my classmates at the University of Cincinnati, especially: Jessica Vozel, Chris Koslowski, Christian Moody, David James Poissant, Leah McCormack, Chelsie Bryant, Ben Dudley, Liv Stratman, Hillary Stringer, Mica Darley-Emerson, Rachel Steiger-Meister, Katherine Zlabek, Peter Grimes, Dietrik Vanderhill, and Jason Nemec. Thank you to Tessa Mellas who is a fabulous magical kindhearted person. Thank you to the other people who have given me good advice, especially Joseph Bates and Michael Nye. Thank you to all of my friends, both human and animal, who have had such an impact on my writing and on my life. Thank you, too, to anyone who I may have missed: The impact on this book by the people in my life is too great to list on this page.

Thank you to Shannon May for producing a terrific piece of cover art.

Finally, I especially want to thank my entire family, from Michigan to Texas to Florida, for their support and love. Thank you to my wonderful parents, Mike and Marsha, who read me books and taught me that *creative* was an okay thing to be. Thank you to my brave and bold sister, Mindy, who goes on adventures with me. Thank you to my aunts and uncles, especially Mimi and John, who have supported and inspired me in more ways than one. Thank you to my lovely in-laws, Trish and Jim. Thank you to Kevin Haynes, who is kind and funny and smart and who makes me very happy.

Baby Baby

There are certain things you keep to yourself. Once, when Mina was ten years old, she went through her older sister's underwear drawer and took her time putting on all of her sister's fancy lingerie, padded bras and lacy silk panties. She couldn't explain it at the time, not even to herself, but she liked the feeling it gave her. It was like trying on a new stage of life, something that is strange and foreign and which excites you in a way that you don't yet have the vocabulary to express. Human beings, Mina thinks, are endlessly odd.

She recalls the lingerie now, as she stands in front of her bedroom mirror wearing a fake pregnancy belly: the heavy, realistic type meant to startle high school girls into abstinence. This, along with the her proclivity for standing very, very close to the bathroom mirror and digging blackheads out of her chin with her fingernail, are things she would rather her boyfriend, Tom, did not know about. And so when she hears the scrape of his key in the lock—they are house hunting, and he's here to take her to another showing—she gives herself one last sidelong glance in the mirror, a small chill of excitement pulsing in her veins as she quickly unfastens the metal snaps and stashes the whole thing in the closet, beneath a wad of old sheets.

Mina isn't sure why she began wearing the belly. She doesn't particularly want to get pregnant, at least not right now. She is thirty-two and has never given much thought to having kids, figuring vaguely that she'll become a mother one day in the way that a lot of women become mothers one day, but that's the extent of it, her future children like a long, dense novel she hasn't yet gotten around to. She bought the belly three months ago to complete the pregnant-nun ensemble she wore to a Halloween party that she and Tom hosted soon after they moved to his city. It was expensive, nearly a hundred dollars, and Tom hadn't wanted her to buy it, had thought the whole thing a bit extravagant, but Mina isn't the kind to skimp on a costume. Halloween, with its witches and ghouls and purposeful trickery, is her favorite holiday. She compromised by choosing the four-month model, a cheaper and more modest bump than the grotesque bulge of the eight-month basketball she'd wanted. They served the punch from a set of hollowed-out gourds and put out white chocolate truffles frosted to look like eyeballs. The party was an unequivocal success.

Then she stashed the belly in the basement locker of their apartment and didn't come across it again until December, when she went down for Christmas lights. She picked it up, put her hands on it gently, like she was touching a woman's body, the swell of an actual baby. It was made out of some kind of thick, dense foam, and when she pressed it the impressions of her fingers stayed for a few moments before fading.

Now, she gently shuts the closet door and meets Tom in the living room. "Hi," she says, standing on her toes to kiss him.

"Hi, babe." He rests his chin on her head. He is tall—almost six-four—and weirdly self-conscious of this fact, but his tallness is one of the things Mina likes best about him, likes feeling his long, long arms wrapped around her, folding her into him, hugging her like he really means it. Not everyone hugs like that.

"Ready to go?" she asks. "I think we're going to like this one. I really do."

He squeezes her hand with his big one, reminding her, unreasonably, of a polar bear. "Let's go," he says.

With the help of their realtor, Laura, they've been looking to buy for almost five months now. They are held back by their own perpetual disagreement: Tom prefers new construction, sharp-angled rooms and taupe walls, but Mina wants something old, wants to feel the history of a place course through her. Tom has been patient and accommodating through the whole thing, letting her make lists of old houses to see and then politely not pointing out the tiny, oddly shaped bedrooms, the crumbling molding, the drafty basements and the old, rattling windows that would need to be replaced. One of the houses had a master suite that could only be reached by climbing up a ladder in a closet; Tom bumped his head on the way up. In another house, a colonial with three perfect bedrooms and gorgeous stained glass in the dining room, they walked downstairs to find the basement flooded with a foot of water.

They drive to the house and wait in the car for Laura to pull up. Buying a home hasn't been quite what Mina expected. She had hoped for a realtor in smart, jaunty suits, who would meet them for coffee to make a long list of their likes and dislikes. Laura is often late and arrives at early-morning appointments in yoga pants and tennis shoes, her face bare of makeup. At first, Mina was impressed by Laura's confidence in inspecting furnaces—*it's old, but looks like it might be in good condition,* she'd say, or *I'd say it's between ten and twenty years old; it may last awhile longer or it may die immediately*—but now, after dozens of houses, Mina has come to understand that Laura is simply evaluating the appearance of the furnaces, comparing the old, massive, jumbly-armed ones to the sleek new ones; Mina feels she could now judge a furnace as well as their realtor. Laura was recommended to them by one of Tom's old friends—Mina can't remember who, if she ever knew—and wonders now if they were somehow duped.

"I like this one," Mina says, after Laura arrives and lets them into the latest house in a rush, flushed with the cold. They walk through the bedrooms, the dining room, the living room, ending in the kitchen. The kitchens are often what kill her dreams of an old house—they are either cramped and old or cheaply renovated, with Formica counters imitating granite and linoleum floors imitating ceramic tile.

This kitchen, at least, has real tile on the floor, real stainless steel appliances. A farmhouse sink. "What do you think?" she asks Tom, who is opening and closing cupboards. They always open and close cupboards, looking at people's chipped mugs, their economy containers of cocoa mix, their cumin and paprika and garlic salt.

"It's a bit—discombobulated," he says. She frowns at him.

"It does need some rearranging," Laura says, surprising Mina. "If you just moved the stove over here, replaced this row of cabinets with a new pantry, put the dishwasher on the other side of the sink . . ."

Mina sees it now, as she never can at first: It's a hasty remodel job, things in the wrong places, the refrigerator marooned in a corner by itself, the best stretch of counter far, far away from the stovetop. "Do you think this house was—*flipped?*" she whispers. She feels shoots of disappointment go through her.

Tom opens the pantry and a half-dozen fat black flies come buzzing out. One of them dive-bombs Mina's hair. She gives a little shriek.

Laura absently swats at one of the flies. "I don't know," she says. And then: "This is the forty-fourth house I've shown you. I think maybe you two need to take some time, talk about what it is you really want."

CSOLO

The first time Mina strapped the belly on she didn't leave the house. She did yoga with it on, got a kick out of performing Downward Facing Dog with the heft of it bumbling around down there, and even imagined telling Tom about it later, the two of them laughing over the silliness of it. But then he'd come home excited about a big sale, had talked fast and happily and taken her to dinner at a nice Italian restaurant and, well, it had seemed like a weird thing to bring up.

A few days later she wore the belly to the drugstore under baggy sweats, sure that nobody would suspect her, but an older woman had smiled kindly as Mina stood in the candy aisle contemplating the bags of chocolate candies, and at the counter a couple of teenagers motioned for her to go ahead of them in line. The thrill of it had zipped through her like a glass of strong beer. She couldn't explain it, not even to herself, but she liked the feeling it gave her. At home she and Tom made wonton soup and then watched an old movie, something with a young Robert Redford. Tom had been none the wiser, and Mina liked that—liked having something that was all her own, apart from the world—something peculiar, maybe, but something known only to her.

෴

Incidentally, Mina doesn't have a job yet. She and Tom have moved from the East Coast city where they both attended college—also Mina's hometown—to the Midwestern city where Tom grew up. *Take your time,* Tom said, and she has: It's been four and a half months, and she's had only two interviews, neither for jobs she had anything but a lethargic, obligated interest in. She has a bachelor's in social psychology and has spent the past ten years working in customer service. It's part of the reason why she agreed, after only six months of dating, to move to Tom's city, to buy a house with him—the pressure of never having done anything in her adult life spreading through her like a cold. And yet it doesn't really matter in any practical sense: Whenever she does find a job, she will earn less than half of what Tom makes at his position in pharmaceutical sales.

She spends a lot of time on the internet. There is a celebrity, a pop star in her late twenties recently married to a prominent music producer, who has recently been under fire for faking her own pregnancy: Invited as a guest on a popular morning show, as she sat down the belly of her dress had billowed and then flattened in a way that caused fans to question whether her baby bump was real. The message boards went nuts. *Guess what people*, wrote JerseyGirl0357, *of course its fake, celebs pretend their pregnant all the time, they don't wanna ruin their bodies.* From mrswilson: *JerseyGirl0357 ur right 100 percent she is definitely not preggo.* Mina feels for the pop star—because when someone tells you that you're not pregnant, takes away the thing that moves and kicks inside of you, what else is left?

∽∘∾

Tom decides that she should begin seeing houses on her own, without him. "Since you've got some—time," he says cautiously. "It makes sense."

Panic rises in her like a plume of smoke. "I don't know," she says. "It feels wrong to go without you."

"I don't mind. I'll go see anything we're serious about before we make an offer."

"That's not really why," she snaps, suddenly angry at him for not getting it, for not allowing her the safety net of his own opinion. Without it she is stranded, marooned, left to form her own poor, misdirected estimations. "I'm terrible at choosing houses," she says. "I like everything. I'll probably pick out a shack for us to live in. Or a hut. Mud will be dripping all over the dining room table, and I'll say I liked the *feng shui* of the place."

"It's not funny," she adds, irritated, when he begins to laugh. His easy laugh, which she'd been so grateful for when they began dating, is beginning to annoy her. *Develop a filter!* She wants to shout at him. *Not everything is funny!*

"Babe, I just think we should move forward with this," he says. "It'll be fine, I promise. Just look at the houses, you know, carefully. Try to notice the details. The stuff we can't see online."

"Oh, okay. Yeah, I'll just be sure to be really *careful*, and that will solve the problem."

She spends the rest of the evening alone in the den, reading celebrity gossip news on the internet: Someone has posted a video of the pop star's baby bump incident in slow motion. When Tom knocks, asking if she wants some ice cream, she says *no* through the door without opening it. Later, when she hears the bedroom door click softly behind him, she waits twenty minutes and then removes the fake belly from its hiding place in the hall closet and brings it back with her to the den, placing it loosely over her midsection.

They end the night without speaking to each other—this is the first time this has happened. He is more upset by the situation than she is, which does not surprise her. When they began dating, a certain imbalance of power was set into motion: He is two years younger than her, which shouldn't have mattered, but which she'd been able to leverage as some sort of relationship capital, the Power of the Older Woman, flirting with Tom for the fun of it, flattering him, until his crush on her took on a power of its own, growing heartily out of its own strength, like cabbage. She'd met him after a particularly bad breakup with a guy she thought she'd marry, a guy she *would* have married had he not told her that she had "stopped being interesting" to him.

Tom is evenly and unvaryingly happy. She has seen him sing karaoke (badly) and participate in a line dance (poorly) without thinking too hard about how he looked. Her old boyfriend had been brooding and contemplative, always worrying over the impression he was making on others. When she brought him to her sister's wedding, he agreed to dance with her exactly once—neither of them were good dancers, and they moved in slow, stiff motions around the dance floor—and she felt a shamed relief when it was over. As the music ended, he dropped her hand like a stone and went to the bar.

In the middle of the night, nauseated by too much television, she goes to the bedroom. She looks at Tom, asleep, his long limbs splayed out on their bed. He sleeps angel-faced, the corners of his mouth turned slightly upward, with the confidence of a person who knows morning will come.

CʒΟᴝ

Once, right after they moved to Tom's city, Mina went on a road trip to New Mexico by herself. She'd gotten ideas about maintaining her independence—they were mostly hanging out with Tom's old friends, and there were no signs of her making any on her own—and she'd planned to camp in the desert alone, bringing along a tent (borrowed from an outdoorsy friend of Tom's—Jason? Jeremy?), flashlights, and a small copper pot for heating up cans of food. When she got to the campground in El Paso there was absolutely no chance of it: Pulling over to scope out a spot, she heard the actual baying of coyotes. Instead, she got a room at the La Quinta Inn and ate half a pizza and an entire row of breadsticks from Pizza Hut. The next day she went to a local crafts fair and perused the large clay pots, old wagon wheels, and hand-woven rugs, suddenly determined to decorate their apartment with some brand of Southwestern flavor. She bought several large tapestries woven by members of the Zuni tribe. But the Southwestern colors, beautiful coppers and cinnamons that looked so vibrant in display, had looked ghastly and overwrought on the walls of their small, pale apartment. She'd stuffed her new possessions into large black trash bags and put them in the garage. When Tom asked where their new décor had run off to, she'd batted his questions away, ashamed at her own indecision and lack of eye for design.

"I liked it," he said. "I thought the art looked good—very *bright*. Lively." This is how he is: a glass-half-full kind of person, heaping indeterminate, generic praise onto everything, as if it were a child's drawing.

"It looked *awful*," she said, and went into the bathroom and cried. A few minutes later she washed her face and came out to watch *Law and Order: Special Victims Unit* with him over frozen yogurt, because you can't explain that kind of thing to a man, crying over burnt orange and sienna.

Three weeks later, she meets up with Laura on her own. The morning after their fight—if you could even call it that—Tom had brought her waffles and orange juice in bed, and she'd been forced to admit that she'd acted a bit silly. Besides, there is a house she wants to see on the city's west side, an old Victorian with an attic office on the third floor. It's an indulgence: Tom wouldn't like it, and he certainly wouldn't agree to live on the west side, with its chain-link fences and greasy spoon restaurants and its areas waiting to be gentrified. In fact, he's so sure of their status as people of a certain neighborhood, a certain part of town, that she is quite certain it hasn't even occurred to him that they might look at houses on the west side—or to argue with her against the merits of this sort of neighborhood (cheap prices, slender, charming streets with real brick houses, diners and independent coffee houses instead of Paneras and Dunkin' Donuts).

She wears the belly to the meeting. Driving toward the location she twice pulls over to remove it from under her clothing, but then she doesn't. Christmas is four days away, and she imagines that the heft on her belly is a gift, a secret present. Since she moved to Tom's city she has not had something that is her own, not even a half-sphere of dense foam.

As usual, Laura is late. Mina has drifted into half-sleep, reclined in her car, when Laura raps on the window. "Sorry," she says, her voice muffled through the glass. "Had to get gas." She motions at the house. "Want to go in?"

The baby bump is only barely visible through Mina's heavy winter coat, but when she removes it in the house's (cozy! charming!) living room, Laura's eyes go immediately to her belly. "Mina," she says. "Oh, my goodness! You're pregnant!"

Mina smiles broadly. "I am," she says, and places her hands on the bump like she's seen the pop star do. In the last week she has worn the belly to the drugstore, the dry cleaners, two afternoon matinees. "*We* are," she says. "We were waiting to tell people, but in the last couple of weeks it's become kind of—well, kind of obvious."

"Oh, Mina!" Tears well in Laura's eyes like little stars. "This is so wonderful," she says, and puts her arms around Mina. "This is so, so wonderful," she says again.

"Thanks," Mina says, after Laura pulls back. "We think it's—wonderful, too."

"Boy or girl?" Laura places her hand on the fake belly. Mina has a fleeting moment of panic—what if Laura detects foam, not baby?—but then looks at the shining happiness in her realtor's eyes. She might as well have a watermelon under there.

"We don't, uh, we don't know yet," Mina says. "I mean," she corrects herself, seeing Laura's brows pull together in confusion, "we're not finding out. We're going to let it be a surprise."

Laura's face relaxes. "Ahh," she says. "I could never do that," she says conspiratorially. "I wouldn't be able to wait to start decorating the nursery. I know it's old-fashioned, but I'd want all pink for a girl. Pink *everything*."

Mina wonders how old Laura is. Older than she first thought—she can see lines beginning to form around her eyes and mouth, and the skin on her chest is lightly mottled with sun spots, like she spent too much time outside as a child. "Oh, are you married?" she asks politely, though Laura's ring finger is bare.

Laura shakes her head. "Chester and I have been together for six years. I'm not the kind of girl to ask questions, but I'm not getting any younger. You know?" Mina nods.

"What about you and Tom?" Laura asks. "Married? Engaged?" She smiles ruefully. "I don't mean to be a prude," she says. "Of course it's fine if you aren't."

"Neither," Mina says. She doesn't tell Laura that Tom has been making noises toward getting engaged, once commenting casually on a display of diamond rings that they passed at the mall, asking whether she preferred round or princess-cut. She doesn't say that when this happened she felt nausea rise in her belly like a wave. She glances around the house, which has blinking Christmas lights drooping from the mantel. "Let's take a look," she says.

CJOLD

On Christmas Day, the pop star releases pregnancy photos. They are tasteful, tropical pictures, the pop star posed in the swimming pool at her sprawling California home, blue water up to her thighs. She wears a candy-cane-striped bikini with little bells on her hips, hands placed protectively on her rounded belly. People claim photoshopping. After they open presents—a fancy coffee maker for her, not a ring, thank god—Mina shows the photos to Tom. "She sure does *look* pregnant," he says.

CJOLD

She and Laura are becoming friends. It is a surprising development, one Mina didn't see coming. The house on the west side had been no good—even Mina could see that, its roof slanting dangerously and the only bathroom crowded by an over-large, pastel bathtub, pink and slippery as a womb—but there have been more showings, meet-ups in the popular neighborhood Tom has his eye on, single-family homes with decks that over-look neat, square yards with landscaping in front and vegetable gardens in back.

They've had little luck with the showings: Mina refused one of the houses after discovering that it had a chimney but no fireplace, claiming it was bad luck; at another, her hands and neck had started to itch unreasonably once she stepped into the foyer. Despite this, they've taken to having dessert together after the showings, Laura placing her hands on Mina's belly while they eat fruit tartlets and flourless chocolate cake, cooing *Baby baby*, saying, *Oh, Mina, you're so lucky*, asking what their birth plan is, whether they've thought of names, how they plan to decorate the baby's room. "You're going to want four bed-rooms now." Laura ticks them off on her fingers. "Master, home office, guest room, nursery. I'll change that on the list." As she speaks, Mina notices that Laura has several raspberry seeds stuck in her teeth.

"Oh," Mina says absently. "Okay, thanks." She presses her fin-gers onto the plate, gathering the last of the chocolate crumbs. She has begun to believe that they'll never buy, that her seeing all of these houses on her own is just indeterminate stalling, or something else.

Cʃᴏᴌ

Except now there is a problem: After weeks of disinterest, Tom tells Mina that he has begun doing his own research online, has chosen an old condo with some renovations (including a real-to-the-touch granite and stainless steel kitchen), a place which even Mina has to admit looks good in photos. He wants to go see it together. "It's perfect, babe," he says. "Old and new, rolled up in one. A good deal, too."

"I just think maybe I should go see it first," she says. "Alone, I mean. Let me form my opinion on my own, you know?"

"Of course." He leans in to kiss her, *really* kiss her, parting her lips with his in the way that he has, a way that is slightly too aggressive, and she notices for the first time that he smells faintly of mothballs. Her tongue goes dry as sand.

"Okay," she says, pulling away. "I'll see the place. And then we'll see it together."

သၢၣလ

The pop star announces that she will give birth on live television. She releases a statement through her publicist: Although she doesn't believe that she has an obligation to share her private life with the public, she doesn't want her future child born in a shroud of mystery and doubt. E! will televise the live birth, interrupting programming whenever it happens.

သၢၣလ

Increasingly, it dawns on Mina that she is in trouble. She has reached the beginning of the period of consequences, the inevitable effects of what she's done: She's seen the condo, and it's good. Good kitchen, good bathroom, good windows, large and bright. Even the basement is good, clean and partially finished, with no flooding. Mina waited, suspicious, for something to go wrong, but it didn't. The whole thing was good, good, good. There's no way to get out of it: She and Tom will see it together, and Laura, who thinks she is pregnant, will be there. Mina realizes that she never thought they would buy a house, that in seeing places on her own she'd be able to taper down the viewings until they disappeared into nothing, like a gym membership you never use.

She makes a decision. She calls Laura, asks if she can meet her at the place a half-hour before she and Tom are scheduled to see it together, so she can have a chance to look at it by herself again. "Fine by me," Laura says.

When Mina removes her coat inside the condo, Laura's lower lip drops a little.

"Mina," she whispers. "Oh, Mina. When did it happen?" She reaches out to stroke Mina's flat belly, but then appears to think twice about it, and leaves her hand hanging in the air, like an injured bird.

"A few days ago," Mina says, eyes downcast. "I wanted to call you, but—"

"Oh, no," Laura says, still whispering, though more loudly now. "Oh, no, Mina. Don't worry about me. I just can't believe it—the baby—" Mina hears Laura's voice waver, and waits for her to go whimpery.

"The baby," Mina agrees, and then something strange happens: Tears fill her own eyes and then seep out, spilling down her face, damp and hot. "Sorry," she says. She is embarrassed by public displays of crying, and turns away from Laura, but she takes Mina in her arms, and Mina presses her damp face into her realtor's neck.

By the time Tom rings the doorbell a half-hour later, the two of them have managed to contain themselves. "If you don't mind," Mina says, after she has washed her face in the sink's cool water, "If you don't mind, don't mention it—this—in front of Tom. He's taking it pretty hard."

"Of course," Laura says. "Of *course*."

The three of them walk together through the condo. The kitchen is nice, with its breakfast bar and professional range-top and sharp, ninety-degree corners, but it is the bathroom that is the true gem of the place: dual pedestal sinks, heated floor, an old, beautiful claw-foot tub. Mina looks suspiciously at the newly installed shower stall, the tasteful glass mosaic tile.

"I like the tub," Tom says. "Don't you, babe?" He puts a heavy arm on Mina's shoulders; she resists the urge to shrug it off. "It's kind of small," she says, about the tub, though it isn't.

"Well—I like it," Tom says. "I like the whole place. A lot. Laura, do you think we could ask for a closing date in February?"

Laura doesn't answer. She is looking at the two of them where they stand in front of the shower, and her lip starts to wobble. *No*, Mina thinks, looking at her sharply, willing her to stay quiet. *No no no.*

"I'm just so sorry for you two," Laura says, and begins to spurt tears. Tom walks over to her, puts his hand uncertainly on her shoulder. He looks back at Mina, who shrugs. "It's okay," he says tenderly. "We're—fine, Laura . . . thanks."

"O-okay," Laura sobs, and then pulls herself together. "You could probably ask for early March," she says, her voice wobbling. "February is a bit soon."

Afterward, in the car, Tom says, "That was weird. Right?"

Mina looks at him, at his head which almost touches the car's ceiling, his adam's apple jutting slightly forward, his nostrils, which are large and flare somewhat when he speaks. She realizes, with indifference bordering on cruelty, that she did not expect things between them to last, that she was soaking up his young attention, his energy, hoarding it and feeding on it, like vitamins, until she was strong enough to go out on her own.

"What?" he says.

Then she opens her mouth, and the words fall out like stones: "It's probably because I've been wearing the fake belly."

He laughs awkwardly, a half-snort, the way you do, Mina thinks, when someone tells a joke you don't understand before you realize that you don't understand it. "Wait," he says. "What?"

"I wore the belly," she repeats, looking not at him but straight ahead at the car in front of them, which has a bumper sticker on it that says *If God didn't want us to eat animals, why did he make them out of meat?* "The fake belly. The one I bought for Halloween."

"You've been wearing it? When?"

"When I met Laura for the showings. She thought I was four months pregnant. I told her we were waiting to find out the sex," she says. "I wore it other times, too. Like to CVS. And the movies."

Tom gazes forward. "I don't understand," he says after a moment. Outside, it has begun to snow. Big, wet flakes stick to the car's windshield.

She is quiet for a moment. "Honestly, I'm not sure I do, either."

They drive in silence, neither of them speaking. The windshield wipers turn the snowflakes to a slush. When Tom pulls into the parking lot of their apartment building, he says, "Mina, that's—well, it's really kind of weird," and then he goes inside.

☙◦❧

The pop star goes into labor. Mina watches the birth alone, in the den. It is the middle of the night, and the snow outside is coming down heavier now, the first real snow of the season. Mina has always been a bit squeamish, and intends to look away during the graphic parts, but she finds herself riveted to the television, watching the pop star moan her way through contractions and then put her legs up into the stirrups, pushing pushing pushing, until finally there is a damp and squalling baby, a happy mother, a proud father.

After the car ride home, Tom didn't speak to her for a couple of hours, staying in their bedroom with the door shut. But then, later, he came to her where she sat watching TV. He took her hands in his and whispered excitedly that he was willing to start trying for a baby, if that was really what she wanted, and this had been so wrong, so absurdly beside the point, that Mina had to keep herself from laughing.

She is leaving Tom, tonight. She is staying at Laura's for a few days and then she is leaving. She isn't sure yet where she's going—maybe home to her East Coast city, maybe somewhere else—what matters is that she isn't staying here. Because how long can you be with someone who sees you at your very worst, who knows the things about you that should be your treasured secrets, that should be held deep inside of you, apart from the world? It's like having your house burglarized, strangers touching your toothpaste and soap. It's like having your insides turned out for everyone to look at.

Her bags, two suitcases and a duffel, are packed; Laura will come back for the rest of her stuff later. She goes into the bedroom to look one more time at Tom, at this man she might have married if she had been a different person, or if he had. Later, she will lie on Laura's long low couch, the two of them bundled in blankets, drinking cheap red wine leftover from an open house. She will get drunk and weepy, and when Laura asks her if she thinks she'll try again for kids, Mina will run her hands over her abdomen, the negative space of where the belly used to be.

But for now she watches Tom, the corners of his mouth twitching, like a rabbit's. She moves toward him, her feet rasping softly against the floor. Tom shifts but doesn't wake. She watches him, thinking how peaceful he looks in sleep, how trusting, how pure and unspoiled by the world. Asleep, he reminds her of someone's little brother, a person who trusts you because he doesn't know any better, who chooses to see the best in you, who thinks you are something you really aren't. Asleep, she finds him very beautiful.

Thank You for the _____

My husband and I are eating takeout spaghetti and meatballs in a motel because our house has bedbugs. At one point we didn't have them and then we did, finding them moving in their slow buzz on the mattress seams and headboard and behind the electrical switch-plate by my nightstand. My husband wanted to stay with friends, but I'm not the type of person who likes to see whether you eat poached eggs or Grape-Nuts for breakfast.

My husband booked the motel. According to him it's *nice enough*, which means it's gross. There was a long dark hair on one of the towels when we arrived and the whole place seems kind of damp, like Spanish moss. The little fridge in the kitchenette works only for keeping beers sort of cold, which we found out after we bought milk and deli meat. The only good thing about the motel is that it has cable. We spend a lot of nights eating cheap Italian food from Paliani's and watching whatever's on: sitcoms, cartoons, cooking shows, infomercials, shows about the lives of famous people's unfamous spouses, shows about people who want to be magicians, shows about badly dressed people who are ambushed into buying new wardrobes. Our favorite is this show about people who have really weird and specific addictions, like a woman who eats baby powder or a guy who spends every night patrolling the streets for dead raccoons and possums to bury.

Tonight we are watching a based-on-true-events TV movie about a woman who donates her kidney to her mother and then asks for it back when she finds out she was adopted. My husband says that's fair, that they should switch the kidneys back and go their separate ways, but I say that when you give something to somebody you can't take that back—that even if you take the gift back the fact that it was given remains, even if it fades over time, like a scar. "They can't just *go their separate ways*," I say.

"It's the thought that counts," he says, "is basically what you're saying."

"No," I say. "That's not what I'm saying at all."

I start telling my husband a story: When I was thirteen I gave one of my friends a bottle of Estee Lauder skin cream for her birthday. It came in a little purple bottle and it looked expensive and cute and when she opened it she thought it was nail polish and I see now how that would have been so much better, because I didn't realize until that exact moment that she had bad skin. She was nice about it, though, thanking me and giving me a little hug around the shoulders, and then we had ice cream cake.

When we were seventeen the same friend gave me marijuana for my birthday. By that point she had a tattoo on her right hip and was sort of arty and good at making stuff, besides being into soft drugs, and she gave me the weed draped in tissue paper and wrapped up in a little ikat-printed bag tied with twine. We smoked it together in her bedroom after her parents went to sleep, exhaling into the cardboard skeletons of toilet-paper rolls stuffed with tissues, and then we ate a jumbo box of Cheez-Its.

"I didn't know you got high," my husband says when I finish my story. We're talking, unapologetically, over the movie now: The daughter has come home, remorseful, and the plot has dwindled.

"I don't anymore," I say.

"Is there more beer?" he asks, and I pass him a sort-of-cold Keystone.

When I graduated from high school my friend's mom hired me to clean her house. My friend was gone by then, in a home for troubled girls in California, because she'd been caught doing coke and because her parents thought she might be anorexic. The job was fair but also deeply personal and sometimes disgusting. Despite knowing this I can't bring myself to tip the cleaning women who work at the motel, who I see every day slouching slowly by with their carts, like bison. When I stopped cleaning her house that fall my friend's mom wrote me a personal thank-you note, though she had paid me generously. It was a good thank-you note, sprawling and kind, words filling both sides of the card and spilling onto the back. When I write thank-you notes it is like a Mad Libs exercise. *Thank you for the* _____, *I am really enjoying it.*

I watch my husband sopping up red sauce with a piece of bread. He is less handsome in profile than he is straight-on, his chin weak and baggy and his nose slightly too large, with a bump in it. I feel suddenly irritable with him. "You know," I say, "they can hide in the spines of books."

He swallows. "What can?"

"Bedbugs."

He turns to me so that he's straight-on, his face now the better version of itself, but I'm already mad. "You think I brought them in?" he says.

"It seems highly possible."

"I don't really ever get books, though." His voice is still mild, unbothered.

"Yeah, I know," I say. "I'm sure they can get in DVD cases, too. It's not like they're like, *Hey, that's a movie, don't climb in there.*"

"Okay," he says, "point taken." And keeps eating his bread.

A few weeks before I stopped cleaning my friend's mom's house I slept with her husband. It happened like this: I thought I was in the house alone, and I went into my friend's old room to snoop through her stuff; it was an irresistible urge I'd had the entire summer. In her top dresser drawer was a little ceramic bowl full of mismatched earrings, a shoebox of folded-up pieces of notebook paper, and some old makeup and a couple of half-used bottles of perfume. The bottle of Estee Lauder skin cream was there; it had never been opened. I took it back: I blew the dust from it and put it in my pocket. That was when my friend's dad came in, startling me: *I didn't know you were here*, he said, and tilted his head at me. *I didn't know you were here*, I said back, and then after that we went up to the master bedroom.

I don't tell my husband this part of the story, but I think about it for a long time later that night, after the movie is over and we've set the TV to the country music video channel and turned the volume down low. I think about finishing the story out loud, telling him what happened, saying this: *I haven't been such a good person, and I guess that's really what I wanted to tell you this whole time.*

Instead I finish my beer and watch Kellie Pickler kick up dust in cut-offs and boots. I look over at my husband: He's on his laptop, trying to guess the password to our online banking account. He is always forgetting passwords, but he won't call to retrieve them until it becomes totally, absolutely necessary—usually when the bank cuts off our debit card because of too many login attempts. "Ah-ha," he says triumphantly. "Got it."

If you want to know the truth I didn't even like my friend's dad that much. He was sort of awkward and he took too long to say goodbye, lingering in the doorway when you were trying to get away, and he liked to talk about this car he had that wasn't very nice. I think he gave me herpes—the mouth kind—because two days after the whole thing happened a sore bloomed at the corner of my lip like a cactus flower. On the other hand maybe it was always there, dormant, under the surface, like something lying in wait.

Planche, Whip, Salto

I.

You spotted the trapeze rig in the spring, where it seemed to have sprouted, like a flower, from its otherwise concrete surroundings. It was pitched on a medium-sized plot of grass in what counts as a park in your Midwestern city, and you passed it as you drove across town to go to the new international food market for ingredients for a complicated Asian noodle dish. You are at an age—thirty-three—at which all of the sudden you aspire to be thought of as a foodie.

It was empty that day: There were no other hints of circus around—no jugglers, no fire-eaters, no high-wire act—and the trapeze looked lonesome there all by itself, nobody swinging into its net, nobody sitting in the half-ring of bleachers that surrounded it. You didn't think about it as you and your husband ate dinner that night, your noodles fragrant with Thai basil and delicious, a rare success (except for two varieties of grilled cheese sandwich, which you do very well, you are not a good cook). But the next week when you drove by, this time with the goal of homemade sushi, there were figures swinging delicately to and fro from the contraption, and you nearly rear-ended the Toyota

23

in front of you. You found the trapeze school on the internet, where you learned that they give performances on Friday nights and lessons on Saturdays. *Experience the thrill of the flying trapeze! All levels welcome!* And so that Friday you dragged your husband to the spot, half-expecting the whole thing to have vanished, like a mirage. But there it was, beautiful at night in the glow of white lights. You took note of the fact that the bleachers were half-empty in only a peripheral way, watching in awe as the aerialists tossed their lithe bodies from bar to bar. "It was okay, I guess," said your husband, who has very specific preferences—romantic comedies with unhappy endings, partially finished basements, steak only if he doesn't have to see it raw first—and then the two of you went out for pizza. But the next afternoon you tied your hair into a ponytail and fished out a pair of old spandex shorts and went bravely back, determined to try this thing for yourself.

II.

You didn't know that it would feel a little bit like sex—the bodily connection, the fitting together of parts—the small *oh!* you released when Isaac, the catcher, grasped you by the wrists and held you swinging through the air, an incredible three or four seconds of weightlessness until he dropped you gently to the net. You didn't know that when the sweet, fresh-faced college student behind you in the fly order, also taking her very first lesson, cried *thank you!* and *that was wonderful!* as she landed on the net after being caught by Isaac that you would know exactly how she felt (amazed, grateful). You didn't know that when Isaac, halfway up the ladder, turned back and said *I want to catch you again* that it would feel like your heart leaving your chest.

He is so beautiful you almost cannot believe it. As a girl you were used to boys who were sweaty and awkward, who you developed crushes on despite their tendency to talk too loud and too quickly, despite their outfits picked out so obviously by their mothers. They were boys whose over-long limbs seemed not a part of them; boys who touched you with clumsy sweaty fingers and then waited eagerly for their turn. At some point these boys became men who worked in marketing and knew a lot about microbrews and played kickball on weeknights, who took you out to reasonably nice restaurants before touching you with clumsy sweaty fingers and then waiting, only slightly less eager, for their turn. With his black eyes and dark curly hair, Isaac is beautiful in a nearly Biblical way: You think that he would not have looked out of place in the Garden of Eden, a banana leaf over his crotch.

You didn't know that you'd be back the next Saturday, and the next Saturday after that. You didn't know that you'd fake severe menstrual cramps to get out of a trip to the vineyards with friends two Saturdays later. You didn't know that you'd take such pure and unsullied pleasure in leaping from a board two stories above ground, in learning how to get upside down, how to arch your back to look for the catch. You even like the terminology that the acrialists use, even before it makes any sense to you, those beautiful strange words: *planche, whip, salto.* Every action of your adult life is a measured, careful decision, even things that are supposed to be fun—what kind of frozen yogurt to buy, whether to go to the movies or rent one on demand—and you take an uncomplicated joy in your uncomplicated accomplishments on the trapeze. *Joy* is not a word you can use to describe any other singular thing in your life. You work for a company that assesses the competency of call center agents—which agents do a good job solving customer problems, which do a poor job, and which do very subtle gradations of jobs in between. None of you, except a plumpish, forty-something woman who always declines your invitations to go for drinks, care anything whatsoever for your jobs.

You didn't know that when you didn't tell your husband how much you love the trapeze that this would feel like a small betrayal, and you didn't know that you'd fall in love with Isaac the way you fell in love with Mike DeCarmo sophomore year of high school—recklessly, carelessly, with the hot spark of adolescence. You didn't know flying on the trapeze would make you realize things about your marriage, like how you wish your husband read books, how you hate that he suspects a conspiracy in everything—even the price of ice-cream cones—how when you're with him you turn into a sly, sneering version of yourself. You didn't know that on the eve of your thirty-fourth birthday, one month after your first trapeze lesson, you would realize that you didn't want children, despite the plan you and your husband meticulously plotted out, the first pregnancy at thirty-five, after you are both established in your careers, the (admittedly small) college savings already socked away. You didn't know that when you told your husband this that he would say *that's okay* and then take a pair of pruning shears to the bushes around your house until they looked small and sad and eventually one of them sort of shriveled up and died. You didn't mean for that to happen.

III.

You didn't know that Isaac would like you back. That he'd notice as your old training from high school diving practice came back, more relevant than you would have guessed, muscle memory returning slowly from wherever it was stored away (forever, you thought) and push you to learn harder and harder tricks on the trapeze, back-end straddle whips and penny rolls and then layouts and double-backs, performing catches with you himself (always), lifting you by your hands your ankles your waist, the two of you a perfect match with your strong lean bodies and dark hair, like brother and sister, almost, except that the parts of your body he touches pulse white-hot for days, until finally the part of you he touches is your lips, and you think you might die, immediately and without warning, from happiness.

But you don't die. You keep flying, every Saturday, except now Isaac meets you some weeknights, too, at the company's indoor rig. You do catch after catch, his hands wrapped firmly around your wrists, and when you finally sleep with him (quietly and urgently, on the trapeze net) it doesn't occur to you that this is a worse transgression than what you have already done.

You didn't know that when the owner of the trapeze company offered you a job that you would accept, that you'd leave your job, your 5 percent 401K match, your seventeen paid vacation days per year, to make thirteen-fifty an hour as a junior-level aerialist at a trapeze school, that in the third decade of your life you'd start anew, having discovered pieces of you that you didn't know existed, sparks and flashes of something presumed long dead. When you tell your husband about your decision he registers the shock quietly, mostly in his eyebrows, and does not challenge you.

On the night of your very first performance, you change into your leotard in a trailer dashed away on the edge of the patch of grass and do your own hair and makeup with the other female aerialists. When you gaze at yourself in the mirror, at your hair pulled back tightly and your eyes dark with mascara, you think that you have never looked so beautiful, not even on your wedding day. Isaac has slicked his dark hair back and when his face appears behind yours in the mirror your breath catches in your throat at his loveliness.

You didn't know that on that night you'd look out into the crowd, glittering with cameras, and see your husband's face. You didn't know that you'd be able to hold his gaze as you climbed up to the platform, hands chalked, ready for Isaac, who waits for you on the other side, and think only of the uprise forward-over you are about to perform. You didn't know that you were the kind of person who would let go of something, but you are swinging now, and there is Isaac, ready to catch you if you are ready to reach toward him, to let his hands grasp your forearms. You didn't know this, but there it is, and there you are.

Rough Like Wool

Nell signed up for the internet dating service because she felt herself caught in a weird kind of limbo: Though she was only twenty-six, the women she knew were either married and planning earnestly for children, or they were single and went out to clubs where they drank watery gin-and-tonics and danced to throbbing music that hurt Nell's ears. At first she worried that someone she knew would see her profile, but then reminded herself that that would mean that he had signed up with the same site. Maybe, even, she would be matched with somebody she already knew, Tony from work or Chad who had been in her spinning class in the spring, and they would laugh about the whole thing and wouldn't even have to tell people that they'd signed up with an internet dating service, but that they'd met at work or in spinning class, whichever was the case. And so she had created a profile and uploaded a photo, vowing to herself that she'd cancel the service after the two-week free trial was up, like Netflix.

She wasn't matched with Tony or Chad but with Peter, who was much older than she was—twenty-five years older, to be exact, nearly twice her age—and he took her to Blue Fin, the nicest sushi restaurant in the coastal Florida town where they lived.

He'd been divorced for fifteen years and retired for six months; he'd been a medical researcher at the local university and was currently a weekly contributor to the health blog on the website of a regional publication. He was also active in a small group of doctors and researchers studying a disease called Morgellons, a newly discovered skin condition, he explained, that wasn't yet recognized by the CDC. When he spoke of Morgellons he was earnest, animated. And yet the night of their first date Nell was able to ignore this feature of Peter's life quite easily by simply choosing not to think about it, like you would someone's fondness for watching monster truck shows or collecting snow globes.

"Of course, my development work with Morgellons doesn't pay," he explained. "But then, I'm not really doing it for the money."

"My job pays—just not very well." Nell finagled a tuna roll with her chopsticks. She had never learned how to properly handle chopsticks, and used them like little swords, stabbing at her sushi prey. "Unfortunately I *am* doing it for the money."

She was a cashier at a beachfront store called The Pelican's Progress, a name that sounded vaguely familiar to her but whose origins she had never bothered to pursue. The Pelican's Progress sold pecan logs and beach towels and shot glasses with the word *FLORIDA!* emblazoned on them. It was a longtime fixture in a town known largely for its research university but which also drew a small, steady trickle of tourists who didn't want to go to Daytona and for whom the Keys were too far away, people looking for an honest little beach town where they could drink Coronas and eat fried shrimp in little beachside restaurants, shoes optional. The town had honesty by the bucketful: The hotels were still the pale pinks and greens of the seventies, with peeling paint and clay-colored roof tiles. The Pelican's Progress itself was charmingly shabby, if that's how you wanted to look at it: The painted-white wood of its window trim had begun to rot, and its sign, a giant pelican that had been wood replaced by tin replaced by a stainless steel mechanism meant to open and close the bird's mouth, had been damaged years ago in a tropical storm and never repaired, so that the pelican's bill was always askew, gaping, as if hoping to catch a fish. Next door was a store that sold vacuum cleaners, with a marquee displaying messages that alternated between humorous and inspirational. The week Nell met Peter, it read *TIME WOUNDS ALL HEELS*.

Because she had no reason not to, she continued dating Peter. They went on a series of outings, to the art museum and the performance theater and to a lot of expensive ethnic restaurants. He revealed that he had a lot of money—he'd lived simply and invested wisely, and now that he was fifty-one and at risk for heart disease felt that it made sense for him to retire; he'd been working for thirty years and he hadn't been to the beach in three, hadn't read the books he wanted to read, hadn't relaxed in years.

He bought her things: new, beautiful hardcover books, a set of wine glasses, the Le Creuset enamel dutch oven she'd been eyeing for months. He paid for her to get her hair colored at an expensive salon after she botched an at-home highlighting kit and came out looking like a demented tiger.

"I think I like him a lot," she told Mandy, her best friend, over frozen yogurts, their weekly ritual. "And he's kind of good-looking, in a Gene Hackman sort of way."

"Oh, Nell," Mandy said, blushing deeply, her skin turning the orangey-pink of a cooked shrimp. "Oh, I'm so happy for you two." Mandy, plump and kind and prone to frequent blushing, had been married for eighteen months to a fat and pleasant man she had met on a singles cruise.

After they had been together for six months Peter paid off her student loans—Nell had been a sociology major in college—and six months after that they were married in a small but exquisite nighttime ceremony with white lilies and candles and a lot of champagne. Mandy, in a peach-colored dress that matched her flushed skin in all the photos, was her only bridesmaid. Nell's parents, retired in St. Lucia, sent a card. Peter's parents, who were dead, did not attend. Nell quickly got used to the idea of her relationship with Peter and the assumptions that came with it: She was a gold-digger, he was a cradle-robber, she only wanted his money, he only wanted her to assure him of his virility, he was having a mid-life (three-quarter-life?) crisis, et cetera, et cetera. She was able to admit the facts to herself quite easily: She was an older man's younger wife. It was an arrangement she had always found repulsive, generally, until she had experienced it specifically, in which case it was quite nice.

But still, it wasn't quite the dynamic one expected. He was rich, certainly, but she wasn't quite pretty enough: Her hair was grayish-brown and flat and her lips were a trace too large and constantly parted, giving the impression of a confused person or a fish. She had a lot of bad habits: She didn't read properly, being too impatient, and when she read the books Peter gave her she often skipped whole paragraphs that turned out later to be of paramount importance, coming to a point where she could no longer understand what was going on and throwing the whole thing down in frustration. Besides that she was an impatient cook, with no interest in measuring cups or tablespoons or instruments that otherwise encouraged consistency, and she soon gave up trying to make dinner for her new husband and instead amassed a great many take-out menus, ordering food from Indian and Greek and Thai restaurants and putting it onto their good plates before they sat down to eat. It wasn't much, but it was more than nothing.

At any rate Peter seemed to love her, emerging from his study in the early evening and kissing her purposefully before sitting down with the paper or a medical journal and a short, heavy glass with an inch of whiskey in the bottom. They had dinner together every night, sitting across from one another at his heavy oak table, a rustic, behemoth thing that sat twelve, and he seemed to derive genuine pleasure from her stories about her old boyfriends, those young, irresponsible boys of her past. Otherwise, they mostly talked about her work.

"Today," she told him one night over baba ghanoush and moussaka, "I sold this woman a postcard that said, *THE WEATHER'S HERE. WISH YOU WERE NICE.*"

He was silent for a moment, then laughed uproariously; he was kind. "More wine?" he asked, holding the bottle over her glass. They drank a lot of wine. In the evenings, after dinner, they watched television together or Nell watched it alone while he used his laptop at the dining room table.

A few months after they were married, Peter began speaking more frequently and more passionately about Morgellons, mentioning small breakthroughs or steps forward that he'd taken in his work, or sometimes simply trying to get Nell to understand what it was he was doing—what the disease's symptoms were, how it manifested, why it was so misunderstood in the medical community. It was a condition, he explained, that was thought by many medical professionals to be a manifestation of delusional parasitosis, a condition that made patients feel like their skin was infested with parasites when there were nothing actually physically wrong with them. There was irrefutable proof that this wasn't the case with Morgellons, he told her, his face becoming flushed and vibrant when he spoke of it, and spent his days in his study doing things that Nell understood largely to be related to the publicity of the disease, of trying to get doctors to understand that it was a real and distinct condition. Often he worked out of his study at home; occasionally he made trips whose purpose she understood inexactly, to the lab or to the offices of colleagues.

The symptoms, as she understood them, were weird: the feeling of balls of hair spiraling down into one's skin, lesions and sores, something or other about malicious fibrous strands. Hearing

Peter speak about the condition, Nell had the impression of being a child listening in on the conversation of adults. Morgellons, she knew, was a thing in his life that she wasn't—and never would be—a part of; it was something that was bigger than her. After all it had been there first, had existed in his life for years before she had, and suddenly she wished that she had a hobby of her own to counterbalance it, like tennis or knitting.

"What does it matter if people don't think it's real?" she asked one night over pork souvlaki.

"Compassion," her husband replied. "Treatment. Insurance. We can't advance our knowledge of Morgellons if people don't think it's real, and the people who have it won't get a proper diagnosis. And, obviously, insurance companies won't cover something they don't think exists."

Nell nodded. She herself was a bit of a hypochondriac, though she recognized this fact about herself. It was a paradox that never ceased to puzzle Peter, though it didn't seem such a mystery to Nell: She knew she was being irrational but was powerless to stop it; wasn't it this way with many psychosomatic conditions, like OCD? She opened her mouth to bring this up but then stopped. Peter had gotten angry the last time that she'd likened Morgellons to her own hypochondria, his face becoming puffed out and red in a way she hadn't seen before, and after that she generally tried to avoid things that would cause this reaction, in the same way that one might avoid giving peanuts to an allergic child.

~

A few months later Nell discovered she was pregnant. They were happy: Peter hadn't had any children with his ex-wife, though he'd wanted them. To celebrate, he took her out for Polynesian food and purchased a large stack of books about pregnancy and childbirth. Mandy bought her an ice cream cake and set of fleecy blankets, tearing up as she held forth her gifts.

It was an easy pregnancy, with the first eight weeks passing nearly symptom-free. She hadn't even thrown up: Once, after fish tacos, she'd felt a small rising in her belly, and rushed to the bathroom, Peter trailing her and holding back her hair as she leaned over the toilet, but nothing happened, and eventually they went back downstairs for ice cream sandwiches.

"Consider yourself lucky," Peter told her when she complained that she didn't *feel* pregnant. "It's a good sign, anyway, having such an easy time of things."

She cut back her hours at work, sitting in Peter's living room and devouring the books on pregnancy, the descriptions of heavy, painful breasts and swollen ankles, of membrane stripping and mucus plugs. Her own breasts stayed small and firm and her ankles slender as a girl's. She began visiting a message board called FutureMommies.com, where she read enviously about the various symptoms experienced by the other women, jealousy filled her insides with something syrupy and gelatinous, like a donut.

But Peter was kind: He massaged her back when she claimed that it ached and held her leg, prepared to rub out a cramp, when she thought one might be coming on. And one night, feeling particularly charitable as she waited for a charley horse that never materialized, she asked him, again, to tell her about Morgellons, feeling a renewed interest in it, with its weird and grotesque symptoms.

"I mean, you've told me what it does," she said. She was lying in his king-sized bed, propped up against three pillows, her legs in his lap. "But you never told me how you got into studying it."

"I didn't?" He stroked her cramp-less leg. "I'd heard about Morgellons patients through the grapevine, I guess. Nobody thought it was real—it didn't even have a name of its own. It was dubbed *Morgellons* by a biologist whose daughter had it, after a description of a 17th century disease that sounded like it could have been the same thing."

"So that's how you found out about it? On the internet?" She tried not to frown; it was in her best interest not to believe things found on the internet inferior.

He nodded. "I'd heard about it from a couple of doctors, but yeah, my main experience with it was through the message boards I found. There were all these people claiming the same symptoms, but they weren't being diagnosed—and if they were, it was with Lyme disease or delusional parasitosis. But they all claimed that they had found these fibers coming out of their skin—they described them as little ropy strands, almost like lint. And so I posted to the message board and asked these people to send the fibers to me. I thought they'd say, 'Oh, they disappear if I take them off my body,' or 'You can only see them if you have Morgellons.' But three days later I got a package, and they kept rolling in after that. From all over the country: Florida, Nevada, New York, Iowa, everywhere. People were desperate."

"You've never told me any of this before."

He frowned. "I haven't?"

She shook her head, lifting her legs off his lap and getting under the covers. She felt odd, unsettled, like she'd had too much to eat—or too little. Maybe it was the jealousy, envy of those with manifested symptoms, filling her insides. Or, it was the people sending particles of themselves to her husband. Maybe that was it. "So these women were sending you pieces of themselves? Like toenail clippings and dead skin and stuff?"

"Men, too, but yes, mostly women. Not toenail clippings. Why would they send me toenail clippings, you goose?" he asked. His face had broken from its stature of gravity that it took on when he spoke of Morgellons, and he flicked her arm playfully.

"Did they include little personal notes? Did they say things like, *Here's my armpit fiber, enjoy?*" She pulled the covers up, so that they came to her chin.

He laughed. "Most did have notes," he said. "But they were about symptoms—or pleas for help. Of course, the most important things were the fibers themselves." He explained that one of his colleagues, Dr. Kelsey, had run them at the lab and found out that they weren't like any other material; they didn't have cuts or extrusion marks that would suggest they were manmade, but they also didn't have internal structures, like cell walls, that would mean they were organic. At 1600 degrees Fahrenheit, the fibers did not disintegrate. They were tough, unyielding, rough like wool.

"What were they, then?"

They didn't know, Peter said. No one knew. But he was convinced that Morgellons was some sort of physical pathology—not a mental disorder or any kind of psychosis. A couple of years ago, a woman, Zoë, had found their clinic, even though they tried to keep their location secret—they didn't want to become a ground zero for Morgellons patients, he explained, they just didn't have the resources—and when Kelsey examined her, he found these tangled skeins of dark fibers like the ones that Peter had received in the mail. "Except the weird thing was that they weren't coming out of lesions or pores," he said. "They were buried in intact skin. They didn't leave any sort of extrusion marks—"

"Nothing?" she interrupted. "Not even a scar, once they were gone?" Peter himself had a scar crossing his upper lip: He'd been elbowed in the mouth playing a game of pick-up basketball years ago. "It gushed quite badly," he recalled when she asked him about it, his hand going to his lip. "I had to go to the emergency room—six stitches." To Nell, the scar was beautiful, dazzling in a gristly, jagged way; this remainder of the life you'd lived; something that would be missing with Morgellons, this necessary, earned memento. Already, she was secretly neglecting to use the special lotion that Peter had gotten for her, a brand heralded for its prevention of stretch marks. She squeezed white globs of it into the toilet instead of rubbing it on her belly and thighs and breasts. She didn't ever want someone thinking that she hadn't had a baby, didn't want to be deprived of this, this thing like a secret wound inside her, a deep, sticky slash written on her DNA, something which made her different from the women who didn't have children.

"Nope," Peter said. "No scarring. There wasn't anything there to leave a scar."

"Did they hurt?" she asked.

"Hmm?"

"Did they hurt? The fibers?"

"Oh." The solemn and faraway look had returned to his face. "Oh, yes," he said. "That's one of the worst parts of Morgellons. The pain."

Nell placed a hand on her pregnant belly. She imagined fibers growing inside of her instead of a child, a slowly unfurling ball of yarn, soft and prickly, pressing against the edges of her flesh, raw and aching and tender.

CSOLO

In June, the heat hanging heavy in the air, like a hand, she insisted that they move. At first she hadn't minded living in his three-bedroom ranch—it was big, sure, several steps up from her one-bedroom apartment, but soon she didn't like the idea of living in the home where he'd existed without her, where he'd spent hours in his study before eating dinner alone at his enormous table and where, she suspected, he was happy on his own. The whole place reeked of bachelordom: the pantry filled with liquor bottles, the black-leather and chrome living room, the framed vintage movie posters, the heavy plaid curtains. She could too easily picture him in his study, receiving packages from strange women with particles of themselves inside, balls of lint and dead skin sloughed off and God knows what else, parceling them out carefully, like little presents, to be sent to the lab.

"I have to be in a place that feels like my home, too," she pouted, rubbing her belly. "Besides, we need a place that has a room for the baby."

He didn't want to move—the market was down; people weren't looking to buy a place like this at a time like this, but she was his new wife and she was pregnant and this made him subject to her whims. He agreed, reluctantly, to list the house, and to their surprise it sold quickly, to another male divorcee in his fifties.

They bought a new place on the other side of town, a luxury townhouse with new construction and a recreation area complete with a pool and outdoor grills, where they often saw their new neighbors cooking their steaks and burgers in swim trunks. He agreed to allow her to decorate, with Mandy's recommendations. Nell felt this was a necessarily charitable thing to allow Mandy, now that she—Nell—was, for all intents and purposes, *rich*, and her oldest friend wasn't.

"Let's start with the living room," Nell said. They stood amidst a mass of recent purchases from several popular home décor stores with names that made it sound like they sold hardware for old ships. Mandy had decided on a tropical motif, and there was a sea of blues and greens in Nell's new living room, a wreckage of chartreuse pillows and seafoam throw blankets. The new furniture had been delivered and set up earlier in the afternoon: There was a sand-colored sectional and a coffee table that looked like a trunk, plus a chandelier in the shape of a birdcage.

"Ohhh, the birdcage chandelier," Mandy said, fingering the wood as if it were gold. She was very charmed by it all, Nell could see. They had the whole weekend to set things up. Peter was away at a conference in Seattle, where he and Dr. Kelsey were giving a paper on Morgellons.

"It's a huge step every time we can present something to the medical community," he'd said. "I'll bring you something back," he said, patting her belly. "Goodbye, Nell. Goodbye, Baby." He hadn't invited her along.

She helped Mandy center a print of the shoreline over the fireplace, against the cerulean accent wall that they'd convinced Peter to paint before he left; after all, pregnant women weren't supposed to paint.

"*You're* not pregnant," he said, looking pointedly at Mandy, before apologizing profusely and agreeing to let them buy the white wicker bench for the front porch that he'd been holding out on.

Nell pulled a pillow out of a bag. It had a giant, embroidered conch on the front. "Are you sure about this?" she said, holding it up.

"I'm positive." Mandy was hammering the frame into the wall with gusto. She was a sturdy woman, and the nail sunk with just a few whacks. She turned to face Nell. "At least I think I am." Her cheeks flushed. "Let's put it all together and see how it looks." She returned the hammer, gently, to Peter's tool chest.

"Do you think it's odd that Peter's so interested in Morgellons?" Nell said after a moment. She was holding a glass vase filled with seashells, banded tulips and wentletraps and lady's slippers, cradling it in the nook of her armpit.

"What do you mean?" Mandy said. "It's his job, right?" Her husband, Ted, was a data analyst for Nielsen.

"Yeah," Nell said, setting the vase on an end table. "Yeah, it is. You're right."

Later, after Mandy had gone home for dinner, Nell stood in her new kitchen, eating crackers by the sink. She'd liked the idea of being pregnant, liked knowing that she could shout into Peter's ear in the middle of the night that she wanted cinnamon toast or black olives and that he'd have to do it, and kept hoping to have untimely and whimsical cravings, ones that they could laugh about once the baby arrived. But she didn't: She had no urges, didn't crave much to eat except crackers and plain white bread, which she snuck downstairs to eat at night, standing up in the kitchen by herself.

She swallowed her prenatal vitamin with a glass of water and sat down on her new couch with her laptop. She devoured the posts with descriptions of symptoms, getting lost in the swirl of pregnancy rhetoric: *My dr wants me to keep track of my TEMP to see if I am O'ing because of the PCOS!☹–Tammy* and *how long were you off the BCP before you were TTC?–DallasGal* She herself had never posted, feeling unworthy of doing so, with no symptoms to share, no complaints of negligent husbands or nosy mothers-in-law. But even so she wanted to—wanted to enter this community of women who were uniquely like her during these nine months. She typed: *I've been preggo for three months but haven't had many symptoms* but then deleted it—that sounded like bragging—and tried again: *my husband is 52 and this is his first child, I hope no one at kindergarten thinks he's the grandpa LOL*—but erased that, too, and went to make herself a cup of hot chocolate.

When she returned, settling onto the new couch with her laptop across her thighs, she entered the Ill While Pregnant Forum. Most of the posts were about morning sickness or gestational diabetes, but there were a few on endometriosis, by women who had posted their stories about trying to get pregnant:

> *Finally I found a doc who agreed to do a lap. He found 5 spots of endo on my right ovary, some in the cul de sac and my bowl was attached to something else. A few months after the surgery the pain came back and he recommended Lupron. Tested pos. three weeks ago! ☺ But still worried about m/c. ☹ —JustineinMississippi*

Nell clicked to reply:

> *I can understand what you're going through, Justine—I suffer from Morgellons. I'm 3 mos. along.—SeaShellNell*

She hit ENTER and then shut the laptop quickly, pushing it away from her as if it had become something dangerous. A rush went through her, the cool heat of adrenaline sweeping her limbs, and she shivered a bit.

She finished her hot chocolate, spooning the dark brown granules from where they stuck, like soot, to the bottom of the cup, and then washed out the cup in the sink, admiring the new living room from her vantage point in the kitchen, her birdcage chandelier and her trunk-as-coffee-table and her cerulean wall. She'd have to remember to thank Peter for that: He'd done an excellent job, being quite meticulous with the painter's tape, the color extending with precision to where the wall met the ceiling or the white wood trim of the windows and never any further. He hadn't made any mistakes; he was good in that way, very good.

When she logged back onto FutureMommies.com there was a little blinking pink baby, indicating that her post had been responded to. She felt a little pitch of adrenaline go through her, a shot of nerves that zipped up and down her arms and legs, and she clicked on her post. Justine had replied:

What is Morgellons? Will it affect the baby?

Nell's hand froze over the mouse, and she felt a real surge of fear for the baby, touching her belly lightly, before she remembered that she didn't actually *have* Morgellons.

*It's a condition that not a lot of people know about, she typed. The doctors are hoping that it won't have any bad effects on the baby, but they aren't sure. The best we can do right now is hope. She paused to read what she'd written, and then continued. *Pls cross your fingers for me!**

ༀༀༀ

July passed in a blaze of white heat, hotter than June, and Nell cut back her hours at The Pelican's Progress even further. She was sleeping a lot, the only visible symptom of her pregnancy other than her belly, which had poked out only enough to make her look like she'd swallowed a large mushroom cap. She was spending a lot of time out on their backyard deck, where she'd let herself sun for fifteen or twenty minutes before getting under the huge umbrella that Peter had set up so she could sit outside without getting too hot. She was out on the deck, leaned back on her elbows, looking at the gentle swell of her belly, rising and falling like a small hill, when Peter burst forth from the townhouse with the news that a national magazine—*Modern Woman*—wanted to do an article on Morgellons.

"One of the doctors who heard my speech in Seattle had a contact, and they want to fly me out for an interview in mid-September. I'll have to go to New York, but I'll only be gone for a couple of days. Will you be okay?"

She struggled to pull herself up onto her elbows, and removed her sunglasses. "This September? As in three weeks from now?"

He frowned. "Well, yeah. But you'll be okay, won't you? I mean, you're barely five months along, and you can call Mandy if you need anything."

"Why can't they just do the interview over the phone?" She looked away, at one of their neighbors, Thomas, who was trimming his hedges into neat, perfect rectangles.

Peter shrugged. "Zoë is going to be there. They want the two of us together, to make a more dynamic interview."

"Zoë? As in one of the women who has been sending particles of herself to you in the mail? Who came from—from wherever she lives, all the way to Florida, to see *you*?"

Peter hesitated. "Nell, this is a good thing," he said gently.

"What did you bring me from Seattle?"

He looked confused. "What?"

"What did you bring me? You said you were going to bring me something from Seattle. Where is it?"

"I gave you the saltwater taffy. Remember?"

"That was from the *airport*. It could have been from anywhere."

He sighed. "Nell, I'm sorry—it was raining both days, I didn't have a lot of chances to get out of the hotel, I—"

She interrupted him. "So there's nothing?"

"Nell, I—"

She put her sunglasses back on and returned to her position on the towel, lying prone on her back, so that Peter was out of her field of vision. "Forget it," she told the sky. "There was nothing I wanted from there, anyway."

☙❧

Her moodiness continued into September, where it settled alongside Saturday afternoons of college football and long walks at dusk. At once it seemed to her that everything Peter did was meant to anger her: He sang songs to her belly at night, quietly, after he thought she was asleep, waking her; he forgot that she liked strawberry jam instead of jelly on her peanut butter sandwiches; he suggested painting the baby's room *olive green*. She became angry at him for the fact that he was, in all probability, going to die sooner than her, and angry at herself that she hadn't given this fact more serious consideration.

"You'll be *sixty-nine* when the baby graduates from high school," she shouted one night over take-out lasagna. She was gripping a breadstick so hard that when she put it down the imprint of her clenched fist remained on it: little sunken, grease-pooled finger marks.

"I *know*," Peter said. This was not the first time she had pointed out this fact. "I'm *sorry*. Please don't harm innocent breadsticks." He put his hand over hers; it was pleasantly warm and dry; the temperature of his body seemed always to be perfectly regulated. There was little that disturbed his equilibrium.

She was visiting FutureMommies.com regularly, lamenting the Morgellons symptoms that Peter described to her, the painful fibers, the cognitive haze, the doctors' lack of knowledge about the condition. Her online friends were wholeheartedly sympathetic: *Nell, what a struggle you've gone through! Pls. continue to update w/ baby news. *Hugs!**

"But you don't *have* Morgellons," Mandy said when she showed her the message board, turning pink with the accusation, but Nell ignored her; she didn't get it at all.

When the article came out in *Modern Woman* three months later, Nell refused to read it. She could see that this hurt Peter, but she couldn't bring herself to open its pages in front of him, to read the words on the page as he loomed over her, grinning stupidly, proud of himself and of Morgellons.

"I'm writing an email to my mom," she said when he approached her with a copy. A big bundle of courtesy copies had arrived in the mail, but she'd left the package on the doorstep for Peter, knowing that he couldn't fault her for failing to pick up a heavy parcel. He'd lugged them in himself when he got home from the lab. "There's some baby stuff I wanted to get her opinion on." She gestured at her laptop. Her belly had *popped*—one of the women at her pregnancy class had told her this was the correct term, that she had passed through the chubby ambiguity of the first and second trimesters—and it stuck out like a basketball cut in half. The space in her lap upon which to set her computer was becoming increasingly smaller, but she'd solved this by sitting with her legs extended, feet on the coffee table.

"I thought we could look at this together."

"Why don't you go ahead—I'll read it later, okay? I promise."

But she finished her email and still couldn't bring herself to look at the magazine. She felt that Peter sensed this but was powerless to take action, and she stayed put on the couch, computer in her lap, and didn't get up to pee, even though the baby was pressing into her bladder, feeling that if she moved it would give him the power to broach the subject again, to put a copy in her hands as she passed by.

It was hours later, when he went out to pick up burritos for dinner, that she picked up the copy of *Modern Woman* that he'd left on the counter, handling it gingerly, feeling that if she only touched it lightly it was as if she had never touched it at all. The article was a feature, a handsome three-page spread appearing near the end of the issue. At his own request, Peter hadn't been photographed, but there were four Morgellons women on the first page, Zoë one of them, and a lot of quotes. *It's weird going in for an appointment and knowing more than your doctor* and *Some of my family members still don't believe that I really have Morgellons.*

She sat down on the couch and logged onto FutureMommies. com, but found she didn't have the stomach for reading the new posts, the mawkish confession of them, weepy like jellied milk. Instead she opened an email that had been flashing, unread, in her inbox for weeks, an invitation from the online dating service to share her experience for a chance to win a $25 gift certificate at Olive Garden. She clicked on the link and began typing into the text box: *When I was matched up with Peter I felt like I was meeting someone I had already known my whole life* but held down the delete key, erasing it, and wrote instead: *My husband is twenty-five years older than me and he's in love with a disease that I don't have.*

When Peter came back with the burritos, she ate hers hungrily, and then she wept, because the food went down easily, without heartburn.

Cʃoʅ⊃

A few days later, he took her out to a fancy dinner and told her that he had news: There was another conference coming up, a half-week in Denver, but this time it was different. It wasn't like regional, like Seattle: This was national—the CDC's annual conference. It was the big one, the conference of all conferences. "Morgellons has never been presented at the CDC," he said. "It's a huge step."

"A huge step," she repeated, this a phrase that had always annoyed her, the idea of a person taking one big, solitary step and then standing in place, like an idiot, until the next thing came along. "But what if I don't feel well? I'm *pregnant*, after all, in case you don't remember." The restaurant was new to the area, and the concept was quite puzzling to Nell: traditional Southern food translated into fine dining, entrees like chicken-fried steak in a balsamic reduction and gumbo made with quail meat. She ordered baby back ribs basted in fig sauce, the most normal thing on the menu.

Peter put one of his hands over hers. "Please, Nell," he said. "How about this—how about I fly into Denver the day I give my paper, and back as soon as I'm done? It'll be less than twenty-four hours that I'm gone."

"You can't keep leaving me to go to these conferences."

"The timing is bad, I know. But I'll be quick. I won't even go to any of the other panels. I'll be in and out. You won't even know I'm gone."

"I definitely *will* know you're gone." She could feel herself getting angry, the blood rising to her cheeks in a hot flush.

"I'm sorry, love. I know the timing is bad, but there's no guarantee that we'll get into next year's conference, and what this could do in terms of legitimizing Morgellons—"

"Let's not talk about it anymore," she said. Their appetizer had arrived: endives with cornbread stuffing. She picked one up and stuffed the whole thing in her mouth, letting the bitterness of the endive dissolve on her tongue. Peter looked like he was trying to decide whether or not she was being unreasonable, watching her eat, smoothing his napkin over his lap several times before picking up his fork.

"I'll bring you something from Denver," he said.

છ૦ω

She began spending the greater part of each day in bed, propped up against pillows, her laptop settled on her thighs. She was becoming increasingly creative in her posts to FutureMommies. com: *The drs are worried that my Morgellons may cause premature labor. Pls keep us in your thoughts. Baby dust to all, SeaShellNell.* She took to eating dinner in bed, from a tray, and often ordered from two or three different restaurants, claiming that she didn't know what she wanted until it arrived. It was a habit that she knew exasperated Peter but which he did not forbid, opening the doors to these delivery men and handing them money in exchange for food. He stopped ordering food for himself, waiting until she was finished and then picking from her leftovers.

"Wait!" she would say as he picked up a cheese wonton. "I was going to eat that."

"I thought you were finished."

She shook her head vigorously. "No!"

Her entire life seemed to be composed of an endless cycle of eating and sleeping. And crying, too—her eyes were in a perpetual state of weepiness; it seemed that any little thing set her off: reruns instead of new episodes on her favorite night of TV, beef instead of chicken in her lo mein, Peter's buying the wrong brand of pink lemonade at the store. Maybe, she thought, her body was preparing her to give birth, returning to this infantile stage so that she might better understand her child.

She didn't want Peter to go to Denver. This, objectively, was not fair: Objectively, a woman should not keep her husband from publicizing a disease whose recognition could improve the lives of people. She repeated this to herself, silently, like a mantra, but it didn't matter: She didn't want him to go. Something seething and acidic began to course through her, souring her insides.

"You'll hardly notice I'm gone," he repeated. "I'll have Mandy come over that night. You two should order yourselves dinner. Anything you want. Make it expensive."

She began taking too-hot baths, soaking in the tub for hours with her belly, slippery with soap, sticking out of the water. The hot water dried out her skin, making it scaly and rough, like a dragon, but she didn't bother with lotion but instead scratched and scratched.

"Honey," Peter said one night after she'd turned her arm red and raw, "Maybe you shouldn't make the water quite so hot for your baths."

"It's not the baths," she said. "I think I might have a *carbuncle.* I saw it on the news last night. Maybe I should go to the doctor."

"Love, I think it *is* the baths."

He encouraged her to go out during the day. She'd stopped working altogether, claiming that she was too tired and too uncomfortable to be on her feet for the entirety of a shift, and so she set up dates with Mandy to get bagels or tea, always choosing cafes or restaurants with Wi-Fi, where she could get on the internet and read the postings on FutureMommies.com. Mandy suggested, timidly, that they might have more interesting conversations if Nell didn't always bring her laptop along, but she was too polite to press the point, and finally gave up and started bringing her computer, too, which she used to go on celebrity gossip sites and read write-ups of the awards shows, opinion columns on how Julianna Margulies or Toni Collette looked on the red carpet. She often showed Nell the reader comments that followed the articles: *I think the problem is did she put her arms in the right holes* and *Who does velvet anymore? Especially that severe, someone help her.* Distracted, Nell murmured in agreement with each of Mandy's own proclamations about hemlines and chiffon overlays, all the time feeling that there was something she'd been denied, something about being pregnant that she'd wanted badly to experience, to feel viscerally, to be a thing of consequence. But it wasn't there; there was nothing there but bagels and websites and your best friend drinking juice because you can't have coffee.

☙◦ℰ

If there was one thing saving her—saving *them*—it was reality television. She and Peter had gotten in the habit of sitting in front of the TV late at night, when Nell couldn't sleep because she'd been napping all day. Their favorite shows were the competitive cooking programs, which they watched with bowls of ice cream or a plate of cookies and imagined, out loud to one another, how good the food on the screen must taste. Nell had the feeling that Peter was indulging her a bit, that he would never have spent an evening this way if she weren't there, and she felt grateful for this, for his efforts toward a common shared thing.

"Mmmm," Peter said, sitting with his arm slung around her shoulders, his slippered feet propped up on the coffee table. "Look at that bread pudding. I bet that bread pudding is really good."

"I bet it's really moist," Nell said. "I bet it's all cinnamon-y and delicious."

"You think cinnamon?" Peter said. "I was thinking more . . . vanilla."

"No way," she said. "Definitely cinnamon. A little bit spicy. Or maybe: maple."

"Maple. Interesting." He kissed the crown of her head and then wrapped both of his arms around her, and she was feeling warm and happy and sleepy when she felt the words bubble forth from her mouth: "I did something bad."

He brushed a strand of hair from her forehead, still playful. "Yeah? What did you do?"

She picked at a bit of crud that had hardened underneath one of her fingernails. "I, uh." She cleared her throat. "I went on a message board and pretended to have Morgellons."

She felt his arm stiffen around her, and he removed his feet from the coffee table. "What do you mean? You got on a Morgellons message board?"

She shook her head. "No, a pregnancy message board. All the women on there were discussing their symptoms, and how they had morning sickness or—or endometriosis, or whatever, and I felt left out, I mean, I—"

"You did this, what, once?" he interrupted.

"A few times." And then: "A lot of times. Peter, I don't know why I did it."

"You wished you had morning sickness, so you pretended to have Morgellons?" He spoke slowly, with a pretense of a person attempting to understand something that could not be understood.

She nodded, still watching the television, where contestants on the show were now racing to extricate the meat from crab shells as quickly as possible, and for the first time it occurred to her that this was a very bad thing she had done—this was a thing that he had a right to get mad at her over, a thing that he *should* get mad at her over, that she'd taken the thing most dear to him and selfishly used it for herself. She wondered, briefly, if this meant she was a bad person.

He stood up. "You know," he said, "people with Morgellons would probably give a hell of a lot to trade it in for morning sickness."

There was a moment of silence, and then he sighed. When he spoke, he sounded tired. "I've got a couple of things to do before I meet with Kelsey tomorrow—do you need anything?"

She shook her head.

"Good." He went into the hallway, and she heard the door to his study shut. It was odd, this dynamic, him being angry with her, and a couple of times she began to rise from where she sat, to go to him. Eventually, she settled back onto the couch, waiting for him to come back. Surely he would come back. But he stayed in his office, through three more shows, and eventually she went upstairs with a box of graham crackers and got in bed.

When the morning came, a week later, for Peter to leave for Denver, Nell refused to get out of bed. In the days after the incident of her confession, she'd tiptoed around her husband, feeling guilty, thinking to herself that from then on she would attempt to maintain some semblance of a good and sane person, but when Peter came in from his study that evening, whistling, and asked if she'd ordered dinner yet, her resolve toward sanity and goodness began to fall away. After her momentary relief over his lack of anger went away, she felt herself slipping closer to a small and unimportant sort of hysteria, an anxious and clinging fear that had become the pattern of their relationship. *He was going to let her do this; he was going to let her be this way.* She wept daily. Peter comforted her, rubbing her back or bringing her cantaloupe slices or chocolate, never asking why she was crying.

The day he was supposed to leave, she was having a particularly bad morning. She'd already made several accusations of her husband, crying out that he was probably glad to get away from her, that he liked Morgellons better than he liked her, preferred its sickly mystery to his own wife. She was lying in bed, wearing his Grateful Dead T-shirt.

Peter was in the bathroom, packing his toiletries. "Love," he said. "You know that's not true." She had a cramp in her belly, a prickly little pain, and as she cried she tried to massage it out, kneading her fingers over her abdomen like dough.

"You're glad to get away from me," she said weepily. Her pillow was wet from the tears. "You're probably not even going to Denver. You're probably going to have sex with that Morgellons woman, *Zoë*. And my belly is hurting and you don't care, you just want to go to Denver, or wherever you're really going, and get away from *me*, from your wife and your *baby*." She was crying again, and turned away from him with a purposeful flourish, so that she was facing the wall, thinking to herself that her behavior wasn't right, it was selfish and unfair and she shouldn't act this way before he left for his trip, but these thoughts went through her head insincerely, without taking root. She heard the sounds of Peter's rustling around the bathroom stop. He came out and kneeled beside the bed.

"Your belly hurts?" he said. "For how long? Why didn't you tell me?"

"I don't know," she said tiredly, and then began to cry again, great heaving sobs, and put her face into her pillow. The crying, all of it, had worn her out, and if she weren't so exhausted it would have saddened her to think that things had come to this, that she was the kind of person who could be truly and emphatically unhappy that the person she loved was going somewhere to do something important.

"Okay," he said. "I'm not going to Denver. I'm taking you to the hospital."

"Oh!" She wiped her nose. "No, Peter. I'm okay, really. Dr. Carey says it's just, uh, *gas*."

He shook his head. "I'm taking you to the hospital," he said.

"But you'll miss your flight. The CBC thing." Her face felt worn, crumpled, like a handkerchief that someone had blown his nose in and then washed. Her anger, which had risen up so swiftly in her, fell away.

"CDC. It doesn't matter." He pulled her up from where she was lying on the bed, putting his hands on her shoulders, holding her there, so that she was facing him. "Nell, I'm worried about you," he said. And then: "We're going to the hospital." He put his hands on either side of her face and kissed her nose. "Okay?"

"We're going to the hospital," she repeated slowly. And then: "Yes. Okay." This, she understood, would be their agreement: He would not go to Denver; he would choose her over Morgellons. It was an act of kindness, one she had not expected, and she began, again, to cry.

He helped her into the car and then drove, faster than usual. Nell felt keenly the irregularities in the road as they went, the little lumps and bulges and dips that came from being driven on for many years, but didn't mind them, feeling that they made the road more lovely for its experiences. She looked out the window as they bumped pleasantly along. Peter didn't speak, and at that moment she felt that this was the greatest gift one person could give another. The pain in her belly was gone, had slipped easily and quickly away, but she didn't tell Peter this, understanding that this was a necessary thing that he was doing, an offering of sorts—these facts were at once very clear: He was doing this for her, he was missing his flight for her, and this was something that had to be done. And she thought to herself, dully, that his acceptance of her, his acting in this way, confirmed what she'd begun to believe, that *this was how she would be*, this was *what* she would be, that her unreasonable and perhaps even deplorable behavior had turned into something irreversible, something hardened and congealed and permanent, that she was like this and she would always be like this and that he would accommodate her, forever. She closed her eyes.

And as she closed her eyes she felt a sensation of rising up, of watching their car travel on the highway from higher and higher in the air, until it was nothing but a speck, a small moving thing carrying two bodies, a man and his young wife, and if you went up even higher you'd see the landscape that surrounded this speck, the palmettos lining the highway and the flat, even grass of coastal Florida, and then at once the peninsula would be nothing compared to the ocean that surrounded it, slow-moving, white-capped waves making their way toward land, breaking onto the shore. Inside the car, splayed open on the floor on the passenger's side, was a copy of a magazine; inside of it was an article on Morgellons, with a picture of a woman named Zoë and of three others, sitting in something that looked like a doctor's waiting room, their surroundings artfully blurred but their faces perfectly in focus, and these were faces of anger, of disappointment, of pain. Nell reached down to pick up the magazine, and she opened it and looked at them. She looked at their faces and wondered what it would be like, to produce these things that hurt you but which left no evidence of this hurt.

A Natural Progression of Things

t's hot. The afternoon is a blaze of sun and slick sweat, the kind Abbott can feel beading up his spine under his shirt as he stands at the edge of the alligator pond, flinging the last chicken sandwich into the water. As he releases it, he lifts his wrist slightly: a small flourish, like a basketball player who has just shot a three-pointer he knows he's going to sink. Then Abbott watches in satisfaction as one of the gators bursts forth from the water to chomp at the food, its jaws open and wide and beautiful in movement. Today there are three of them: long and thick-tailed, with skin that is cracked and gray. The two on the left bank are large, probably twelve-footers at least, the third a baby gator: smaller, quicker, ever so slightly less dusty-looking. A mother and father and their kid, Abbott thinks. A little alligator family. He feels something like a measured affection for the gators. Once, visiting the pond mid-afternoon, he'd seen a couple of redneck kids creeping toward one of the gators with a stick, poking its scaled back, and he'd been glad, actually happy, when the gator made a sudden lunging movement that sent the two boys tripping and scurrying back up the hill.

He comes here most afternoons, after he gets off work at the Chikin Shak. He brings sacks of old chicken sandwiches and cups stuffed with curly fries, containers of cole slaw and brownies past their sell-by date. He likes to think that the gators look forward to his visits. "You really shouldn't feed those gators," his house-mate, Gwen, has said. "It makes them associate people with food." The wooden sign posted at the edge of the nature trail concurs: use caution, it reads, and below that, somewhat more pedantically, *This is not an amusement park*. But it's no under-statement: There is no fence between the pond and the trail, only a dip in the hill culminating in a sunken pool of water at the bottom, edged in loblolly pines that cast shadows on the ground that the gators slink under on hot days. But there is only the one sign, and it is quite small: The people of Florida are casual about their gators. *You're on your own*, the sign's subtext seems to read. *Don't be an idiot*.

But Abbott's always been a good kid, and he never ventures past the last of the pines, tossing sandwiches at the alligators from the edge of the walking path. He hurls a handful of curly fries in the direction of the smallest gator, most of the fries falling in the water closer to the two larger gators, who move toward them without lifting their snouts from the pond's surface. One of the large gators slaps the other's tail playfully with its own, as if to say *It's my turn*, and Abbott watches as the two of them take turns snapping up the fries. He crumples the paper bag in his fist and tosses it in a nearby trash can. *I'll see you guys later*, he thinks, but he doesn't say this out loud. He isn't crazy.

CROLD

At home there is a gift waiting for him on the kitchen table: a large, rectangular object wrapped in the Sunday funnies. He rips the paper off. There are two things inside: an oblong metal tin and a book with a Post-it stuck to its cover.

Saw this and thought of you.
Gwen

The tin is full of chocolate-covered pretzels. The book is a hardback, glossy and new, a picture of a large gray-green alligator on the cover. The title is a speech bubble coming out of the gator's mouth: *When Alligators Attack: Recorded Fatalities Since 1970.*

The two of them, Abbott and Gwen, share a duplex, though they didn't know each other when they moved in. This, the knowing each other, came later, hinging on small, neighborly requests—did Abbott have a light bulb she could borrow, and could he hear that banging in the laundry room at night or was she completely fucking nuts? The duplex did not originate as a multi-family dwelling; rather, it is a two-story house split in two, a thin, rattle-prone sheet of drywall installed at a rough midpoint on each of the floors, ostensibly allowing for two separate parties to share the building. The problem is that a house intended for one party is not easily split into a house occupied by two. The kitchen has landed entirely on Gwen's side of the house, the living room on Abbott's. He has a makeshift pantry—a wobbling set of shelves where he keeps pallets of peanut butter crackers and stacked boxes of instant macaroni—and a hot plate in the corner of the living room, sitting atop a stool borrowed from the breakfast bar on Gwen's side. His half of the house is bare, bare, bare. Gwen has decorated her side with care, dressing the downstairs window with curtains and even setting a row of potted purple hydrangeas on the windowsill. From the outside the house has the look of a lady with one heavily made-up eye.

Abbott is nineteen, a sophomore at the community college, an undeclared major. Gwen is thirty-two and a student at the university across town. A freshman in status, she is unapologetically closemouthed about her years-long hiatus between high school and college. She is short, brunette, with an evocative gap between her front teeth and a large rear end. She wears big, dangly hoop earrings and owns matching windbreaker-and-pants suits in several different bright colors. Abbott thinks she is beautiful. She is majoring in art history but, Abbott knows, dreams of publishing cookbooks, particularly of baked goods. Now she is working on her first book: a compilation of sweet and savory pretzel recipes. She spends her evenings making batches, packing samples of them into shoe boxes stuffed with bubble wrap and mailing them to publishing houses. "They've got to taste the goods," she argues, and though this seems odd to Abbott he doesn't complain. He is often on the receiving end of the pretzel overflow. This is what composes the second half of his gift: a cluster of white-chocolate-covered pretzels drizzled with dark chocolate and sprinkled with toffee bits. Abbott takes a bite of one, letting the bittersweetness of the chocolate dissolve on his tongue.

There is a knock, *rap-rap-rap*, from the other side of the wall. "Hey," Gwen says. "Abs, is that you? Come over."

Abbott opens the thin wood door that separates their sides of the house. Gwen is sitting on a stool at the bar, watching her tiny television and reading a gossip magazine. Her pants are shiny and maroon. "Did you get my present?"

"Yeah." Abbott blushes.

"Did you like the pretzels?"

"Yeah." He is still cradling the tin in his left arm. "They're beautiful."

Gwen beams. "Thanks," she says, turning a page in the magazine. "I thought it was an especially good batch." She gets up and fills a glass of water from the tap.

Abbott smiles in agreement. He looks at the magazine—*Us Weekly*—splayed indecently on the counter: JENNIFER LOVE HEWITT TO PAPARAZZI: "QUIT CALLING ME FAT!"

"I couldn't resist the book," she says. "I saw it on the bargain rack at the bookstore. I thought it was really cool, like, let's catalog death and not pretend that it doesn't happen, you know?"

"Yeah," Abbott says, nodding. "Definitely cool. Very cool."

Gwen sips her water. She is wearing a blue T-shirt emblazoned with the image of a palm tree and the words *Jimmy Buffett for President* across the chest. Abbott imagines saying something witty, maybe "Where does Jimmy Buffett stand on homeland security?"—but thinks better of it. He desperately wants to impress Gwen, a feat that seems increasingly impossible as the weeks pass.

She is looking at him. "I heard it again last night," she says. "The noise."

Abbott's tongue feels thick in his mouth. "I didn't hear it," he says. He's always been a heavy sleeper.

She smiles. "Well, you're going to have to do something about it," she says, and she is being coy now, flirting with him in a way that makes him feel like he did when his mother left him with his old babysitter, Jill, a large, blond teenager who used to walk about the house in a bikini, her breasts half exposed, persecuting him with her sexuality. Abbott often finds that Gwen reminds him of Jill, though she is neither large nor blond. Also he has never seen her breasts, though he wouldn't object to doing so.

"I hope I hear it tonight," he says stupidly.

"Yeah," Gwen says. "Me too." And then: "I think I'm going to turn in. See you in the morning, babe." She folds her magazine in half and takes it with her, her thighs swishing as she makes her way up the stairs to her bedroom, until she is out of sight.

ᴄᴊᴏʟᴐ

This is Sandy Springs, Florida, a coastal town an hour from the smaller, more central town where Abbott grew up. In addition to the midsize university that Gwen attends, there is the community college, which, Abbott has heard on the local news, is actually quite reputable. It is one of three schools that admitted him and the only one that offered enough financial aid for him to attend. Abbott likes the school well enough, as he likes most things well enough. Two out of his four professors seem to know his name, which, to Abbott, seems pretty good. The town itself is filled with hardworking people who hit the beaches for rum drinks on the weekend, people generally united in agreement concerning the superiority of the university's football team. There are good barbecue restaurants and pretty girls. The town is amiable, sunny. Abbott likes it well enough.

He has one friend: a boy named Eli, who sits beside him in Introduction to Psych and works at the grocery store next to the Chikin Shak in the strip mall. Eli sometimes agrees to go with Abbott to the alligator pond if they get off work at the same time, which Abbott likes because it means that he gets to ride home in Eli's car, a decrepit orange hatchback with a rusted-out frame, instead of walking. Now, the two of them stand together at the edge of the nature trail, tossing chicken and fries to the gators, Eli explaining to Abbott how a person might go about knowing whether a customer will request paper or plastic.

"I get it right nine times out of ten," he says. "No bullshit. It's like, the more of a tight-ass somebody is, the more likely he's gonna want paper, because plastic is small and it's flimsy and it's just not good enough for him. So I see a guy come through the checkout with pre-cut vegetables or frozen lasagnas—convenience food, you know?—and it's like, I know he's not gonna mind plastic because he's cool, he doesn't care about that sort of thing. But you see a lady yelling at her kids to be quiet and quit touching the candy bars, and it's like you *know* she's gonna want paper." He stops and considers this for a moment, an empty bun in his hands. He tears a strip of bread off slowly. "I guess that's not exactly right," he says. "If she's *yelling* at her kids, she might say okay to plastic because she doesn't have time to concern herself with what kind of grocery bags she's getting. But if she's *whispering* in their ears and gripping their arms and telling them to behave themselves in public, she's paper for sure." He nods, satisfied with this assessment.

"That's very interesting," Abbott says, his mouth stretching into a yawn.

He is tired: The night before, he tried valiantly to stay awake, waiting to hear the sound. Half a dozen times he was almost able to convince himself that he'd heard something and ventured out into the hallway only to be met with silence. He had made it two-thirds of the way through the pages of the book that Gwen had given him, which were incongruously filled with beautiful, scenic shots of alligators—one of a snout breaking the surface of the water in a Florida lake, another of dozens of sets of yellow gator eyes shining in the dark—and blocks of text detailing reported deaths by gator.

☙❧

Lorelei Steele, 87, female. Mrs. Steele's body was spotted floating in a retention pond 500 feet (150 m) behind her daughter's ranch-style home in Lake Charles, Louisiana. An examination of the stomach contents of the reptile in question conclusively established that Mrs. Steele had indeed been attacked and killed by an 8-foot (2.4 m) alligator.

☙❧

The listings were mechanical, disturbing in their cold, statistical report. Abbott had felt deeply bothered, a sensation of unsettlement snugged up in his chest when he finally fell asleep.

"I tried to explain it once to this dude," Eli is saying. "And he cut me off and said that he preferred paper not because he was a tight-ass, but because he had discovered that they were *the exact size of the inside of his kitchen trash can*, and he could use them as trash bags. Now, who but a tight-ass measures the inside of his trash can?"

"No one," Abbott agrees. He looks down at the water. One of the gators is sunning itself on a rock. Abbott watches as another dives underwater, surfacing to nudge a third gator's tail with its snout.

Eli flings a hunk of chicken at the water, where one of the larger gators snaps it up before it hits the surface. "You and that girl," Eli says. "The old lady. I know that's what you're thinking about."

"She keeps hearing a sound," Abbott says. "In the house. She wants me to do something about it." He adds: "She's not old."

"Then *do* something," Eli says. "Christ. She's practically asking for it."

"She's not asking for anything," Abbott says. "Except for me to find this sound."

"Then find the sound."

"I'm *trying*," Abbott says, thinking that Eli doesn't get it at all but at the same time knowing that he is right, that he has to find the sound, take care of it, because what other splinter of hope, of opportunity, might come his way in the coming months, before he and Gwen relinquish their leases and part ways? He must make a statement of purpose. He must find this sound.

"I know," Eli says. "We'll go by my apartment before I take you home. I'll get you a couple of my brother's pills. You'll be able to stay up all night."

"What pills?" Abbott asks, alarmed. He does not like the sound of these *pills*, something consumed by Eli's brother, a thirty-year-old high school dropout who suffers from hyperactivity and possibly a variety of other malaises as well.

"Relax. It's just Adderall." Eli looks at Abbott curiously. "I'm trying to help you out."

"I know. Let me think about it." Abbott turns back to the pond, tossing a whole sandwich into the water on the far side of the smallest gator's sunning rock so that it might get a bit of food. Before eating it, the alligator tilts its head slightly in his direction, as if in gratitude.

⌘

It's hot again: one of those nights where even the wind that blows through the window is warm. It's a tropical breeze, the sort Abbott has felt on his skin all his life, but tonight it irritates him that the night air is sticky instead of cool, that it makes his shirt stick to his back and puts a flush in his cheeks. Abbott looked Adderall up on the Internet after accepting the two oblong red-and-white capsules from Eli, weighed the dangers of taking someone else's prescription drugs against the potential benefits. Side effects, it seemed, included emotional lability and stomachache. Abbott didn't know what emotional lability was, but he swallowed the pills anyway, with orange juice, and went to his room to wait.

And so when he hears a faint scratching noise at a quarter to four, he is far from sleep; has, in fact, paged twice through the death-by-gator book and eaten all of the chocolate-covered pretzels. Abbott entertains briefly the possibility of entering Gwen's room to address the noise, to comfort her—surely she would appreciate his concern, his can-do attitude?—before setting the book carefully down and holding very still. Sure enough, there it is again: a scratching sound, louder this time, and a bumping, too, coming from beneath the house. Abbott drops the idea of waking Gwen and leaves his room quietly, ears wide open and listening. He thinks of Sam, his boyhood pet, a brown-and-white beagle whose investigatory skills were unparalleled.

Abbott makes his way down the staircase and goes quietly through the door into Gwen's side of the house. It is something like passing through a portal into another world: His side of the duplex, depressing in its sparseness, has lately become dirty and crowded with trash—he has been letting cola cans pile up in a large white trash bag in one corner of the living room, and there is a pile of unfolded laundry in the middle of the floor—while Gwen's kitchen is prim, feminine, clean. On the kitchen counter sits a fake begonia potted in real dirt, as if with enough encouragement it might someday take root and grow. The gesture strikes Abbott as thoroughly optimistic.

He follows the bumping and scratching into the laundry room, where it is more pronounced than in the rest of the house. He puts his ear to the vinyl floor and listens—maybe there is an animal caught in the crawl space under the deck? Standing up, he notices that two of Gwen's bras have been left to dry, hung up on nails hammered into the wall above the washer and dryer. They are sturdy, substantial bras, made of white cotton and without unnecessary flourish. Abbott can imagine that this sort of undergarment would be appropriate for a woman like Gwen, who never wears revealing clothing and who, he is pretty sure, hasn't undressed in front of a man in some time. He chides himself silently for the thought, his ears growing hot at the idea of Gwen naked.

Making his way outside and letting the screen door shut softly behind him, Abbott walks down the three wooden steps that lead from the deck to the backyard and circles around the side of the deck to where he can get on his knees to see underneath. He clicks on the Maglite he has brought with him, light filling the space below the deck. He takes a quick, fearful step backwards at what he sees: a large raccoon nested within the space, using its paws to tear siding from the house where it has been made loose with waterlogging and rot. Abbott can see that the raccoon has already made considerable progress in the construction of a makeshift den, strips of board forming a loose pile next to the animal. As if sensing Abbott's presence—or perhaps seeing the beam cast by his flashlight—the raccoon turns accusingly before returning to its task, its eyes like two black marbles set deep in a mask of fur.

Abbott puts up a hand in apology. "Sorry," he whispers, slowly making his way to his feet and backing up. He walks back to his bedroom. He is thinking of Gwen, how she looks in the sweatpants and gray T-shirt that she wears to bed, and of the raccoon, its small, cold eyes, its humanlike paws, remarkable in their dexterity. He thinks to himself that there are two kinds of people in the world: those who take action and those who don't. The people who take action get paid good salaries to do the jobs they want. They get their teeth cleaned regularly and they return library books on time. They get out of stale marriages, end friend-ships that have soured. They kiss the people they want to kiss.

People who don't take action, like him, generally wait for others to do it for them. They forget to return phone calls. They wait for their parents, teachers, bosses, and best friends to tell them what to do. They don't complain when their steaks come out medium-well instead of rare. Sometimes, he thinks, good things come to the non-action-takers and sometimes they don't. Sometimes wonderful, lucky things come and the non-action-takers turn them to shit with their poisonous, lazy touch. He tells himself he will not turn this to shit. He will catch the raccoon and woo the lady.

❧

Since it's only a quarter mile from the beach, the Chikin Shak gets a steady stream of beachgoers seeking a lunchtime reprieve from the sun, coming in wearing bikinis and flip-flops, their hair-lines wet and pushed back and sandy beach towels tied around their waists. Abbott serves them chicken sandwiches and curly fries in red plastic baskets. He hands them Styrofoam cups of icy lemonade made from lemons that he prepped that morning, cut-ting them in half before putting them on the juicer, one in each hand, methodical as hell, *bzzzt, bzzzt, bzzzt,* down to the rind, filling up a nice four quarts of juice to dilute and mix with water and sugar and ice before selling it for a buck seventy-five a pop. He keeps a cup of the stuff next to him as he works the grill, the cool sourness of it feeling good on his tongue, keeping his mind off the hot steam that rises from the metal plates as he presses the chicken breasts on them until they sizzle.

Eli has come in for his lunch break. Abbott sneaks a cup of fries that Eli didn't pay for onto his tray. It has been a bad day at work: Abbott woke up that morning with a headache settled deep into his skull, his sense of hearing so sensitive that it hurt to listen to his own voice repeat orders back to the customers. Keenyah, the owner's daughter and the restaurant's day manager, rode his ass so hard that Abbott had to ask to be put in the back, where he could work the grill. He is struggling there, too: He keeps over-cooking the fries, screwing up orders. He twice forgot to dip the chicken fillets in milkwash before dredging them in flour, causing the breading to fall off once they went in the deep fryer.

"Abbott, I want you to tell me how come a grown man can't remember to pound out this chicken *before* breading it," Keenyah said, marching over to show him a fillet that hadn't been ade-quately pounded before it was breaded and fried, so that instead of a nice, even slab of meat there was a gnarled lump of chicken, knotted and curled up on itself like the fist of an old man.

Now, with Keenyah in the back office cashing out the day-shift registers, Abbott allows himself to lean on the counter, rest-ing his elbows on either side of the cash register. Eli stands at the counter eating his food; it is nearly three o'clock and there are no other customers.

"I've got a plan," he tells Eli. "I know what I'm going to do."

"Let's hear it."

"Well," Abbott says. "Gwen is worried about this sound, right?"

"Right."

"I'm going to take care of it," he says. "It's a raccoon—I saw it last night. All huddled up under the back deck. I'm going to bait Sam's old crate and get it, then take it out to the preserve to release it. And Gwen will finally be able to get some sleep." As he speaks the words out loud, the plan sounds better and better to him, and he tosses a fry in the air with flourish to finish off his speech.

"That's a stupid-ass idea." Eli drags a fry through ketchup. "Don't be retarded. You can't catch a raccoon."

"Can and *will*," Abbott says, feeling more confident than ever, a rush of exhilaration sweeping through him palpably, from head to toe. Perhaps it is a latent effect of the Adderall. "I'm going to keep staying up until I can do it." He takes another fry from Eli's tray and tosses it in the air, catching it in his mouth. He chews and swallows. "Can you get me some more pills?"

ଓଠ

Eli comes through for him: He gets more pills, enough to last Abbott a couple of weeks. Abbott borrows Eli's car to make the hour-long drive to his parents' house to get Sam's crate, waiting until his parents are at Wednesday-night Bible study to punch in the garage code and sneak the thing from under a pile of loose two-by-fours, tin cans, and other items that his father felt necessary to keep for future home-construction projects. Abbott's backup plan, in case they were home, was to tell them that he is transporting a puppy for a friend. His father is a stern, conservative man who pushed hard for Abbott to join the navy after graduating from high school; he would certainly not approve of his son's partaking in novice raccoon-catching. His mother is kind and a bit naïve, often wondering aloud why Abbott didn't attend more homecoming dances and pep rallies in high school. She understands little, Abbott thinks, about social strata. Sneaking the kennel from the garage, though, he is almost regretful to miss his mother. She would listen to Abbott describe Gwen, would think Gwen *sweet*, as she does most girls that she suspects as objects of her son's fondness. But he keeps his eyes on the road as he drives off with the crate in the backseat, anxious to reestablish the fifty-mile buffer zone that will keep him from an actionless existence, a comfortable existence, one free of rent and full of consistency and completely devoid of Gwen.

ᘓⱺᘒ

There's a problem, though: The raccoon refuses to enter the crate, becoming even more destructive and bothersome than before, making terrible screeching sounds at night and uprooting the herbs that Gwen has been attempting to grow in a small, square plot in the side yard. Once, Abbott manages to lure the animal successfully into the crate by baiting it with a string of purple grapes, only to have it tear back out before he is able to shut the gate. He has shown the raccoon to Gwen, has tasted the satisfaction that came with her thankful recognition that he had at least *identified* the problem, a feeling that cultivates a hunger to *solve* it, particularly when Gwen complains, one night, that the raccoon has continued to torment her.

"I'm tearing my hair out, Abs," she says over plates of spaghetti and a movie, a late-eighties action flick with Patrick Swayze. They are sitting on the floor in Abbott's living room, eating off paper plates. "That thing is keeping me up at night. It's eating my *basil*. Really, did you ever hear of a fucking raccoon that ate basil? Of course it doesn't touch the weeds."

I guess it has a refined palate, Abbott wants to joke. He has opened his mouth when Gwen speaks again.

"Abbott," she says. "That raccoon has to die."

Abbott slurps up a strand of pasta, wiping red sauce from the edge of his mouth with a paper napkin, waiting for her to say that she is kidding, that she is frustrated by the inconvenience, sure, but that of course she doesn't wish death upon an innocent animal.

But she doesn't say this. Instead she continues. "You know what we're going to do? We're going to trap that raccoon and feed it to those goddamn gators." She makes a chomping motion with her arms, not unlike the motion used by fans at athletic events undertaken by the university's sports teams, whose mascot is an angry-looking green alligator.

"Circle of life," she says. "What were you going to do with it, anyway?"

Abbott shrugs, thankful that his mouth is full of pasta, because honestly, he hasn't considered this, hasn't let his imagination run past the moment of gratitude that will surely come when Gwen sees that he has trapped the animal.

She shrugs back at him, then smiles. "I'm telling you," she says. "It's what we've got to do. And anyway, you can show me these gators that you're always talking about."

❧⊙☙

The next night, at the pond, Abbott is sure that the alligators know what he is thinking. He sits cross-legged at the edge of the trail, tossing chicken to them, trying to reindulge in past fantasies about Gwen's thankfulness of his bravery in solving the raccoon problem, fantasies now marred by the messy, uncomfortable notion of death. He pictures Gwen, shielding her eyes from the glare of the setting sun as she watches the gators, smiling at Abbott, thanking him for bringing her, because wow, this is really cool, and when else do you get to see nature so up close, so vivid, so *real?* But this image is replaced by one of the raccoon, busying itself tearing at the siding, its black eyes meeting his brown ones before it returns to its work. At once Abbott is struck by the sadness of destroying something so industrious, so primitively intelligent in its instinct to construct a protective shelter for itself and—he nearly shudders at the thought—its young. *Stop it,* he tells himself, standing and brushing the dirt from his palms. He has thrown the last bit of chicken to the gators, and he tosses the crumpled paper bag in the trash can before he leaves.

❧⊙☙

When he gets home, Gwen calls to him from the back deck, where he finds her drinking pink wine from a juice glass.

"Abs," she says. "Come join me."

He takes a seat next to her in one of the four plastic patio chairs that surround a matching table. It occurs to him that the deck, as well as the rest of Gwen's half of the house, is in want of visitors it has never seen—the guest towels awaiting overnight company, the silk-flower centerpiece on the dining-room table, the decorative citronella candle sitting atop the patio table. Gwen is eating pretzels, milk-chocolate-covered ones, with stripes of caramel and coconut flakes.

"Hi, Gwen," he says, reaching out to take a pretzel.

"Get some wine." She gestures with her glass. "Drink with me," she says, her manner as casual as it might be if they had a glass of wine together each night, as it might be if Abbott were not nineteen years old and had never tasted a drop—not one drop!—of alcohol.

Her mouth widens into a smile and she pushes her tongue up against the gap between her front teeth, and at once Abbott is standing up from his chair, remembering his resolve to take action, is going into the kitchen and opening the refrigerator and pushing down the black spigot on the box of wine sitting on the top shelf, filling a tall glass with the clear pink liquid. He gulps down a mouthful of the stuff in the kitchen, preparing himself for the worst, the wine surprisingly sweet on his tongue. He tops off his glass and goes outside. The sun has begun to go down, long shadows from the lounge chairs falling across the deck.

"Attaboy!" Gwen says. Abbott takes another careful sip of wine, letting the liquid fill his mouth before swallowing it down. He looks into his glass, making a gentle circling motion with his arm and watching the wine swirl around in the glass. He gulps a mouthful down, and then another. On the table the citronella candle has been lit and gives off a sickly-smelling smoke, gray and curling. He watches the smoke, dissolving as it rises into the air.

Gwen is talking about a movie that she's seen, something with Sandra Bullock. "And so then he regains his memory," she is saying. "But it doesn't matter, because she's already in love with the brother."

"Yeah," Abbott says, and he is feeling good, feeling even stronger in his resolve to take action, feeling that sitting here, drinking wine from a box with Gwen, is the absolute best thing on earth that he, Abbott, could be doing at this moment. He takes Gwen's glass and goes into the kitchen and refills them both, the wine sloshing a bit as he carries the glasses back to the deck, where she thanks him without noticing the spillage, or without mentioning it.

The sun has dipped below the horizon now, is nothing but a smear of orange in the distance, Abbott watching it and thinking how beautiful Gwen looks with her hair tied loosely at the back of her neck with a band, when they hear the noise, a scratching and clattering that comes from directly below them: The raccoon, Abbott knows, is inside the crate.

"There it is," Gwen says, her chair tipping dangerously back as she starts at the sound, and Abbott knows that she, too, is feeling the wine, is unsteady, he hopes, in the beautiful, wonderful way that he is unsteady.

"Yeah," he says, and his voice sounds amplified, magnified, just plain *loud*, as the words leave his mouth. "It's in the crate. I'm going to catch it," he says unnecessarily. And then: "For you."

Gwen grins at him. "You wouldn't kid a girl."

Abbott grins back. "No," he says, standing from his chair, bumping his wine glass, so that even more sloshes out the top, setting it on the table in front of him and sliding his hand into an old leather gardening glove—his only means of protection from the animal's teeth. He moves silently down the steps, motioning for Gwen to join him by the side of the deck, where he leans down to peer into the crawl space.

"Hold this." He hands her the Maglite, which she holds, no questions asked, watching as he approaches the crate.

"There he is," she whispers, the glint of the flashlight illuminating the raccoon's backside, its ringed tail catching the light.

"How will you close the latch?" Gwen asks.

"I'll just have to reach over and shut it," Abbott says, "before it has time to get out." He keeps his eyes on the animal.

"What then?" Gwen whispers.

"What do you mean?" Abbott says, his eyes still on the raccoon, which seems, like everything else, to be moving in slow motion.

"What will we do with the raccoon after we catch it?"

Abbott looks at her dumbly, his tongue thick and dry in his mouth, his head starting to hurt again from lack of sleep. He has tried, again and again, to avoid thinking about this moment, to consider only the feeling of triumph that will necessarily accompany his catching the raccoon. But now, looking at Gwen, the fact of the raccoon's fate is unavoidable.

"We'll take it to the gator pond," he says simply, the words barely out of his mouth when the raccoon makes a quick bumping motion, one that causes Abbott to take action with a surge of speed he didn't know he possessed, lunging at the crate with the gardening glove, his hand pushing the gate shut and the tip of his pointer finger pressing down on the latch with just enough force to trap the animal inside of the crate, a small hissing, whining noise escaping its mouth and the raccoon looking at him, terrified, a single grape between two paws, and Abbott thinking dizzily that even if he is trapping this raccoon and potentially feeding it to an alligator, at least it will have some grapes to eat.

Gwen turns to him. The flashlight, still in her hand, droops, making a circle of light on the ground below. "You did it," she says. In her other hand is a glass of wine.

"Yeah," Abbott says, gesturing for her to hand him the glass and taking a long drink, feeling confident now, feeling good, unstoppable, like this is it. He puts both hands on her shoulders. "Can I borrow your car?"

ᘓᓪᓄᘔ

They drive to the gator pond, Abbott behind the wheel, his head pounding now, everything happening too slow or too fast, the raccoon in the backseat making horrible snarling noises and clawing at the crate's metal gate in a way that makes it feel like the whole car is rattling, the dark outside getting even darker, Abbott focusing his brain power singularly on keeping the car in the correct gear, on steering it around the necessary turns. It is a short drive, and they reach the preserve quickly. Abbott gets out of his side of the car, walking around to open the door for Gwen before he— *carefully*—removes the crate with the raccoon inside and sets it on the ground. They are at the edge of where the land dips down toward the gator pond, and Gwen peeks cautiously at it from safe ground. "So these are your gators," she says.

Abbott smiles. "They are." He can see the tip of an alligator snout as one of them glides gracefully through the water, the tranquility of its movement giving Abbott hope that the inevitable doesn't have to occur, that perhaps the gators have had their share to eat for the day—after all, wasn't he here earlier with plenty of chicken sandwiches?—that somehow this, the earlier feeding of the gators, absolves him from what he is about to do.

A set of gator eyes catches the moonlight as something, an animal, makes a sudden movement, a rustling in the brush that surrounds the pond, and he feels Gwen's arm tighten in his.

"So," Abbott says, his arm tingling where she is holding it, feeling like it has a million nerves in that exact spot. "These are, you know, *gators*, which is also the mascot for—"

"The university," Gwen finishes, a smile breaking on her face. "Living here must give them an extra sense of purpose."

"Yes!" Abbott says. "Yeah. Exactly."

They stand quietly, and there is nothing more to do now except to *do it*, and so he moves toward the crate, takes a breath, and *one-two-three* makes a quick lunge at it, putting his finger on the metal latch to set the animal free and thinking, *No, no, I can't do this*, and then feeling his finger push down, just enough to spring open the door and release the raccoon, which rushes out, only turning its head toward Abbott momentarily before racing into the brush, moving toward the light of the water. *No*, he thinks. *Not that way*. But he is undeniably hopeful, too, guiltily buoyant as he returns to Gwen, who puts her arm through his.

They stand, looking at the water, arms linked, Abbott wanting to pull her closer and at the same time not wanting to move his arm away from Gwen's, not now, not ever, when there is a loud rustle in the brush below, and it is only for a split second that Abbott sees the raccoon, so that later he won't even be able to say for sure that he saw it, but knowing that he did, and knowing that Gwen did, too, before he sees the gator that lunges for it, its jaws closing on the animal in one quick, deathly motion, and then opening and closing its mouth in three, four, fatal chomps before swallowing it down, the sound of death loud and terrible and undeniable, and Gwen is taking his hands now, both of them, and then he is kissing her, her mouth hard and wet against his, and he is closing his eyes and he is still kissing her, the moonlight that he can't see reflecting off of the water, reflecting off of three sets of yellow eyes below, still now, as beautiful as anything he's ever seen.

The Men

This is how Addy likes her life arranged: power yoga on Saturday mornings, jogging on Tuesday nights, reality television no more than three nights a week. Two close friends: Ellen, who is sarcastic and good at baking, and Jennifer, who likes everything, even bad movies. Addy alternates Thursday nights spent with the two of them, like a special kind of yin and yang. She has a pleasing little job: She is the assistant of a woman named Judy McNamara, a stylish, seventy-something ex-academic who is writing a book on the history of contraceptives. Judy pays her way too much to take notes on the use of the acacia bush as sperm deterrent by the ancient Egyptians or sometimes to brew a pot of coffee or spread cream cheese on celery. Addy sometimes suspects that Judy is mostly interested in her company, and perhaps in a younger woman's views on the Nuva Ring. The work is secretarial, mostly, but she enjoys it; thinks maybe someday she'll do something as interesting as what Judy McNamara is doing. *Greek gynecologist Soranus recommended jumping backwards seven times after intercourse to dislodge sperm.* She comes up with little ideas from time to time, and pitches them to Judy, hoping she'll recognize a faint glimmer of talent and encourage Addy to take on her own interesting, feminist projects.

She also has a boyfriend: This one's name is Cole. Having a boyfriend is important, because Addy takes great joy in her relationships, which she prefers to last between two and six months. She is the kind of girl men do things for: Jerry, a pastry chef she dated for six weeks, had delivered personalized sweets to her door each weekend, little soufflés and dainty cakes with her name iced on top among sugared hearts. Blake, a divorce lawyer with thwarted musical aspirations, learned how to play the sitar, and composed for her a sweet and dreadful song. And then there was Grayson, who, inspired by the Larry Walters documentary the two of them had watched together, traveled by lawn chair in helium-flight at fifteen thousand feet above earth for her—and even when he accidentally dropped his pellet gun to the earth, startled by the pop of the first weather balloon (which he shot as a means of beginning his descent—a descent that was supposed to culminate in the courtyard of the apartment complex where she lived at the time) even when he was picked out of a tangle of tree branches and power lines by a rescue crew with a crane and arrested for entering an airport traffic area without authorization, Addy knew that, like the rest of the men, Grayson found his own actions to be not overwrought or injurious but terribly, terribly romantic.

Addy loves being in love, likes waking up next to a man in the morning, thrills at seeing a sturdy, manly toothbrush next to her delicate one. She's a serial monogamist, moving from one man to another like a person might switch breakfast cereals; loving one intensely until suddenly you hate it for being so sugary and for leaving crud on your teeth.

Possibly more than the men themselves, Addy enjoys breaking up with them. She collects the discarded men in her head, lines them up in neat rows and columns like presidents, their likes and dislikes and occupations and weird habits engraved on her brain. And she thinks fondly back on them, feeling that they in some way still belong with her—*to* her—these boys in their por-traited memory. She likes to think of them by themselves in their one-bedroom apartments, apartments with dirty sponges, with posters of sports teams taped to the walls for decoration, apart-ments that called out for the trace of a woman: here a lacy bra hung on the doorknob, here a rumple of lingerie left on the night-stand. And she doesn't think them mean, these little fantasies, only honest, a picture of a man without his girl.

She has told Cole about the men, about the gestures. She always discloses her dating past to her current boyfriend, but in a way that makes him feel that his actions are somehow different: more momentous, or less momentous, or something.

But Cole has hung around longer than most. He is proving difficult to get rid of: When she took him to the rock gym, plan-ning on breaking the news after they'd taken turns belaying each other on several of the walls, he looked so darling in his climbing gear, clapping out excited little puffs of chalk when she reached the top of the intermediate wall, that she lost her nerve.

He likes camping, and this is why Addy has brought him here, to Cumberland Gap National Historical Park, to dump him: To her, a breakup is like a work of art, a performance, the swan song of a relationship. She plans on remembering this breakup, on savoring it, like it was a book she was forced to read in high school but only later realized the value of, though still in a vague, clouded way, like looking through the frosted glass in her grand-mother's bathroom window.

But now, watching Cole pitch the tent, bending the fiberglass poles into delicate arches and raising the fabric of the tent from nothing into a shelter, she feels the familiar ache of affection—she's always loved men who could successfully put things together, a skill that strikes her as primitively masculine—and she has to remind herself that he has to go, really, he leaves used tea bags around her apartment and he cleans his ears with Q-tips *in front of her* and besides that during the half-mile hike to the campsite he kept pulling things off of trees and saying "are these blueberries?" before eating them, grinning at her the whole time, and she told herself, half-heartedly, that she wished he would just drop dead right there so she wouldn't have to deal with it, the whole breaking up thing—but the wish departed quickly, like a wisp of something, a sneeze that never comes. Of course, the breakups are the best part.

"Sky's starting to cloud over," Cole says now, fastening the rain fly. "We might get some water tonight."

ભ•

She is going to break up with Cole in the morning: First, they'll have a good, strenuous hike to the summit of the mountain, where she'll give a little speech about why things aren't working out. Endorphins, she thinks, will soften the blow. They'll go back down the mountain and pack up the tent and make the hour-long drive back home, which might seem like it would be awkward but is a part of the breakup that Addy takes a great satisfaction in, the denouement of the thing, a deep, warm feeling of sorrow settling in and taking root, and she savors this pain, feeling that what she and Cole, or Jerry, or Grayson had must have been something, really something, for them to now be sitting here looking at each other in this teary way, and half the time swears to herself that she'll retract her words, though she never does.

"Did you look over the pamphlet I gave you?" Cole, finished pitching the tent, rolls out his sleeping bag and gets inside. He zips himself up so that only his head is sticking out. She thinks to herself that he looks like a jack-o-lantern poking out of a cocoon.

"About dehydration?" She yawns. "Yeah." She gives her bag a resounding pat. "Three liters."

"No. About the—" He lowers his voice. ". . . about the—*bears*."

"Are you afraid they'll hear us talking about them?"

He pokes her in the side. "Don't get smart. This is *bear country*."

"Don't worry," she says. "I know a lot about bears. This guy I knew? He came face-to-face with one. He told me all about it."

"Really?"

"Really. He and a friend were hiking in the woods when they came upon this huge, mean-looking black bear. It reared back and roared at them, like it was ready to attack. So the guy bent down, got his sneakers out of his backpack, and started putting them on. His friend said, 'What are you doing? You can't outrun a bear.' And the guy said, 'I don't have to. I just have to outrun *you*.'"

"That's not funny."

She'll miss Cole, sure. He's got a bundle of good qualities: Besides his adeptness at pitching a tent, he also makes a mean breakfast sandwich. He's a fantastic cuddler, wrapping her in bear-hugs that are vigorous and jovial, not the polite and unconvincing grasp of some men. But Addy has to dump him, you see, because she's begun to have impulses that she doesn't understand. She's been thinking about taking a class in making mosaic-tile furniture, or maybe going skydiving, and she thinks she might like to be single for a while.

It's not the first time she's felt this way: Right after college, she dated a boy named Stephen Datlow; a *man*, really, is more right to say: He, Stephen Datlow, was older than her by eight or nine years. He was her very first serious boyfriend, and she'd begun dating him in what seems now like it must have been a different era of her life, a time before the urge to systematically and creatively break up with men seized her like a disease.

Stephen Datlow was trying to *get into music* around the time that they started dating, and she broke up with him at the symphony, whispering the words into his ear between movements. She wore an expensive, intricately beaded gown and red lipstick. The whole thing was quite beautiful and sad, and they held each other all night before she left his apartment in the morning. Her preserved image of Stephen Datlow suddenly fuzzes in and out, like a television with bad reception, and Addy frowns a little, so surprised is she that she hasn't thought of him in so long. He liked spicy food, she recalls, would order the Paad See Iew hotter than he could stand it and gasp, "God, that's good," while eating it, in a way that always slightly disgusted her; he was into food politics and often wrote passionate and detailed letters about the lack of social responsibility in the grocery industry that no one published. They fought when she accused him of not respecting her job as a supermarket cashier, and again when she became temporarily unemployed after quitting theatrically when her manager demanded that she pay for a crate of peaches she'd dropped.

Stephen Datlow was the first man she'd ever broken up with. The experience had been quite exquisite: He'd broken down in tears, right there at the symphony, sobbing and begging, and it had been like a high, a potent sensation of her own capability. It was downright addictive, that feeling, though she tells herself that this, the feeling, is not the reason she is breaking up with Cole; it can't be, surely, that would be downright *shallow*—and hedging dangerously on *bitchy*. Something, a small gem of discomfort, floats down through her and settles in her gut, like sediment. She closes her eyes and inhales deeply, trying to shake it off.

"Did you know," Cole says now, inching his sleeping bag toward hers, "that during the Civil War, soldiers used to spoon at night? For warmth?"

"How did they decide who got to be the big spoon?" Addy says, and Cole laughs and pulls her to him.

అఠఠ

In the morning, Addy wakes to the warmth of a pleasing little fire and to Cole setting before her a tin plate with three strips of bacon and a piece of plain toast. There are hulled strawberries and a big thermos full of coffee.

"Crunchy," she says, biting into the toast, and he grins at her, his mouth full of bacon. They set out on their hike, her heart fluttering a bit to see him in his gear, his slouchy pocketed shorts and sweat-wicking T-shirt and a special bladderlike water bottle that has a tube that goes from his backpack into his mouth.

"I had an ex?" she says. "He really liked playing dominoes, but he hated the outdoors. He never would've made it to the top."

Cole gives her ass a solid smack. "Good thing you're with me now."

The trail cuts through a gently sloping hillside of purple spring flowers and then climbs, switchbacks leading them over paths that become narrow and rocky. They follow it over mossy rock, Cole going first and reaching back to help pull Addy up after him. Addy drinks from Cole's water pouch. Cole uses his knife to carve their names into a tall pine: ADDY + COLE. Addy takes his picture next to a plaque explaining the passageway's strategic value in the Civil War, thinking that maybe she'll keep this picture in the drawer in her desk at home, where she'll pull it out from time to time and think of Cole, caressing the memory of him like an old blanket. She will remember how good he was at putting things together and how tightly he hugged her, she thinks, and something twitches in her heart, pulls and tugs a bit, so that when he announces that he's going to wander off the trail to take a leak in the woods she asks if it's okay if she goes on without him. "Go ahead, babe. I'll catch up." He shields his eyes and looks up, toward the summit. "It looks like we're not too far, now, anyway."

ᘓᔓᘐᔑ

At the peak a heavy white mist hangs in the air, making Addy worry for the visibility of the pre-breakup photographs she'd planned to take of her and Cole together. What should be a beautiful vista of the charming, historic town below, as explained by another plaque, is lost in a cloud of haze, thick as cotton. She begins to think of what she will say to Cole, and a little tear wells up in her eye; a comfortable, familiar feeling of sorrow begins to settle in her gut. She snaps a photo of the plaque. *It's not for a lack of love, Cole. It's about me finding things out about myself. It's about me getting to know* Addy.

She thinks back on the other men she's broken up with, the speeches she's given, the delicate and nuanced performances she has delivered. She thinks of Grayson, who she broke the news to at the apex of a hot-air balloon ride. She remembers David and Jeremy—she broke up with them at a U2 concert and while the wedding cake was being passed out at a wedding, respectively. She imagines her impending breakup with Cole, sees a stirring speech delivered at the top of a mountain: tears, an impassioned exchange of words. Maybe even a sobbing refusal to get in the car with her, or, *even better*, a threat to take the car and leave *her* behind, alone on the trails of Cumberland Gap National Historical Park. A little chill of excitement goes through her at the idea.

She watches Cole as he comes up the path below her: This part of the trail is full of switchbacks, turning back on itself in sharp angles before curving toward the mountain's peak, and she has a good view of him as he nears her. It occurs to her to wonder what *his* grand gesture would have been—a gesture that hasn't come to pass but certainly would have, she's sure of that, had she not chosen to end things at this time and this place. He's done things for her: Just that day, there'd been the breakfast, the names engraved into the tree, but there has been nothing *big*, nothing *gratuitous*, nothing grossly exaggerated and theatrical, and it occurs to her that the occurrence of these, the gratuitous and the theatrical, have been, for her, an assumed good. She watches Cole as he gets nearer to her, swallowing a ball of something,

something that feels dry in her throat, like doubt. She puts her hands together in a little clapping gesture as he approaches.

"We made it," she says, her voice catching a bit in her throat.

"We made it!" He puts her hands around her waist and lifts her off the ground, twirling her in a full circle before placing her on her feet again. He gestures at the space before them. "Where are the cheering fans? The orange segments? The bagels?"

"I think there's a Panera three or four miles after we get on the highway. But we've got to go back down first."

"No, I meant—you know, like when you finish running a 5K and there's—never mind." He kisses her head. "Good job you. And me. We made it."

He flicks open his knife and approaches a tree to begin, again, to carve their names. "Last time," he says. "This way we'll have one halfway up and one here. To commemorate our journey."

She watches him put the blade to the tree, pressing the tip of it into the wood to make the first incision, like a surgeon, *A* for *Addy*. It seems to her a bit sad, but also beautiful, this carving away of the tree's flesh, and she remembers something Stephen Datlow once said to her, about the carving of sculptures: *The art is already there; you've just got to peel away the excess.* She'd laughed at this statement, thinking it ridiculous and false and stupid, and telling him so. She shakes her head a little at this thought; she doesn't want to think about Stephen Datlow right now, but there he is: a polite and unconvincing cuddler, but a genuinely kind man, lover of animals and generous tipper of restaurant staff. He made a respectable amount of money. He had good hair—he had *great* hair! *Why* had she broken things off with Stephen Datlow? Of course, there had been the feeling of the breakup, the great sensation of emotions poured forth on her behalf, but it had to be more than that—didn't it?

Watching Cole, she remembers another thing about Stephen Datlow: He fancied himself a painter, had practiced his craft all over the walls of his apartment. A whole side of his living room, she remembers now, was covered in a mural he was working on. The mural was not only an exercise in color but one in texture, too: raised lines of red and orange, like bumpy rivers, swirling around a huge mass of color in the middle of the wall.

"What *is* it?" She'd asked one night, when it occurred to her that the mural might actually *be* something. It was a massive organ of some sort, it seemed, this realization coming to her after she'd looked at the thing dozens of times. And she had remembered then that he'd dropped out of med school before he began selling insurance and producing odd and amateurish forms of art, and the realization of this fact became part of the identity that she projected onto him: a failure in the hard sciences, forced into the banal and boring, in need of a savior of sorts. And, incidentally, she saw herself as this savior, she who saved him from eating fish sticks for dinner and who was kind enough to play Scrabble with him afterward, though quite honestly she found the game to be a drag and spent most of the time trying to arrange her letters into some variation of a dirty word.

Stephen Datlow took her hand and put it on one of the bumpy rivers, traced her fingers over its path as it traveled the length of the wall, to the tangle of lines in the mural's middle. "This is an artery," he said, and moved her hand to a smaller bumpy river and then a smaller one. "Vein. Capillary."

She didn't speak, just stood there with her fingers on the purple capillary, trying to decide if it was the best piece of art she'd ever seen, or the worst.

"I call it 'Archaeology of the Heart,'" he said, and she kissed him so that he wouldn't keep talking.

Now, the memory of it gives her a pang, because she managed to nearly forget the mural altogether, a fact that surprises and disappoints her, the sparkle of the story she'd once so treasured gone dull, tarnished and imprecise. Her memories of Stephen

Datlow have come back to her in a fractured, disjointed kind of way, little shards of recollection floating about like amoebae: She can't remember what he liked in his coffee; she can't even remember if he *drank* coffee. She wonders if this is what will happen to her memories of Cole, if she will fail to remember his Q-tips, his water pouch, the little grunts he made as he pitched the tent. Something inside her quakes and teeters, like a portrait falling from the wall and shattering. And then it happens that she can't remember at all what it was she wanted to say, the eloquent and touching little speech she'd planned slipping, draining away, until it is gone.

"I'm going to wander this way and take a couple of pictures," she says, jerking her head to the right, toward a small clearing in the trees. "Be back in a sec."

"Sure, babe."

She begins to walk away, but turns back and gives him a little hug, squeezing him around the waist fast and hard. He shuts his knife with a click and puts an arm over her shoulders.

They hold this pose for a moment before she slips out from under his arm. "Be right back. Then we'll head back down?"

"Sounds good."

She walks over to the clearing and raises her camera, pointing and clicking haphazardly at the mounds of cloud before her. She kicks at a stone on the ground, hurting her big toe. There is a sensation of hollowness in her belly, as if someone has removed all her organs and replaced them with air. She thinks again of Stephen Datlow, trying hard to remember why it was that she'd broken up with him, thinking that if she can recall a good reason—one single, solitary good reason—then she will be saved, that it won't be the fact of the matter that she has traded something real and good for the pleasure of a resulting story, an amusing little narrative. She thinks hard: It was the way she ended up lying on the couch, bored, while he played video games after dinner, maybe?

Or!: the mural. Surely it was the mural. She watches Cole pick up a rock, examine it, and put it in his pocket. He catches her eye and waves. She waves back, feeling sure that if she were to look down into a pool of water that her reflection would have suddenly aged thirty years, her skin creased and eyes wrinkled with a newfound burden of knowing things. She walks to the railing and stands there, looking out onto the land between mountains. The fog has not cleared, and all that is there is white, white, white, as if there is nothing at all.

Grip

I love the pole vault because it is a professor's sport. One must not only run and jump, but one must think. Which pole to use, which height to jump [. . .] I love it because the results are immediate and the strongest is the winner. Everyone knows it. In everyday life that is difficult to prove.

—Sergey Bubka, 1988

When Ewan began pole vaulting again, he did it secretively, furtively, a thing he held inside his chest until it pulsed—like a family secret, or a lie. Lucky for him, it was a sport well-suited to solitude: You didn't need someone to hit ground balls to you, to rebound missed shots, to return your serves. It had been eight years since his last vault—it was hardly a sport of casual pursuit—and he missed it. Really missed it. Standing at the end of the runway before his first jump, he felt a build-up of energy course through his limbs, the sensation so visceral that he closed his eyes and simply let himself feel the weight of the pole resting in his hands, that lovely feeling of anticipation. It was the day after he and Cora decided, officially, to start trying for a baby, him making a nervous joke as she pulled him to her that it was time to see if his boys could swim.

He has been vaulting since he was fourteen, a skinny high-school freshman who joined the track team with his cross-country buddies only to discover that he was a hell of a lot better at getting upside down on a pole than he was at chugging out 3,200 meters around an asphalt loop. But it's more than that: He loves the sport for its technicality, its grueling sequence of choreographed movements. It's an art form: way better than the tasks performed by blockheads who try to keep other blockheads from hitting their quarterback. Better than guys whacking at a ball with a bat or a racket or their hands. A year into vaulting, he came to think of most other sports as some form of Neanderthalism, half-convincing himself that he wouldn't have wanted to play football even if his mother hadn't forbidden it—or if he had broken the buck-twenty mark on the scale. To be successful in the vault, he reminded himself, one has to be precise. Meticulous. A pole planted in the box a half-second too late means being yanked under, an unsuccessful swing, bad penetration, a failed vault. And yet there is room for interpretation, too, arguments among elite vaulters over whether the bottom arm should be locked against the pole or allowed to flex, about whether one should follow the Petrov model or the tuck-and-shoot. It is a sport like no other: transferring the pent-up energy of one's runway speed into a vertical jump with a piece of fiberglass that floats you sixteen, seventeen, eighteen feet into the air . . .

Once he took his first step down the runway it was as if he had never stopped vaulting. He wasn't as fast, sure, but the movements were there, his drive knee lifting automatically as he leapt off the runway, his body inverting in a beautiful and fluid motion. It was as if his brain were able to shut off, so that he was thinking of nothing at all. To him, this seemed a delicate achievement, one that might not withstand the company of another person. He doubted Cora would see it this way: She'd want to know why he hadn't felt he could share this with her—in college, she loved watching him vault; why couldn't she come, too, to watch him fool around at the track?

But what he's doing isn't fooling around. Pole vaulting is a sport that simply cannot be taken lightly, nor practiced casually. It takes *cojones*, requiring of its participants a cocky headstrong quality without which one ends up at best unsuccessful and at worst injured…or dead. He learned this, really learned it, his freshman year in college, after showing up hungover to a six a.m. practice: If your takeoff lacked the proper aggression—if you failed to show the pole proper respect—it would turn on you, your momentum stalling you in the air for a moment before the bend in the pole snapped back and landed you on your ass, or worse. He spent six frustrating weeks of the indoor season with a boot on his foot for a fracture that should've healed in three.

And so Ewan knows this. Knows the risks. Knows that vaulting solo eight years after the last meet of his senior year is probably unwise. Taking the runway with a pole that isn't his with rusty mechanics and unconditioned muscles—it's more than dumb: It's idiotic. Moronic. Cora wouldn't say these things, but they'd hang in the air, unspoken: She's trying to get pregnant, which means this would be a bad time to injure himself. *They* are trying to get pregnant, she'd corrected him once, earlier that week. It is a joint deal, a thing that takes two: a duet, a square dance, a game of checkers. *A boxing match*, he thought to himself.

But that first time back—it was almost too easy. He arrived at six-thirty, long after the high school's athletic teams were done with practice but still an easy hour before the sun would disappear into the horizon. This isn't the high school he attended— he's from Indiana; the southern Tennessee city he and Cora have settled in is familiar to him only from the perspective of college student and then alumnus—but he knows it well: As a member of the university's varsity team, he was one of a handful of student-athletes who agreed to help coach the track team at an area high school. And so he knew that they kept the key to the equipment shed under the slab of black rubber that sat at its door, knew that the poles would be inside, resting on a gargantuan set of welded metal shelves built by the school's shop class. Stepping inside the shed for the first time in years, he inhaled deeply the scent of must and dirt, feeling only a brief twinge of nostalgic guilt for the time he'd spent pushing lanky and uncoordinated high-schoolers onto the mat before quitting the gig because he had turned twenty-one and gotten a girlfriend and—quite honestly—just hadn't felt like doing it anymore.

Now, vaulting has become a weekly habit. And he's gotten brasher with it, too, spending less time doing run-throughs and plant drills and more time just straight-up vaulting, doing a five-step approach and seeing how high it takes him. His run's a bit off, and he knows he's not inverting as well as he could, but his plant feels damn good, confident and sure, and he's getting good penetration into the pit. He has yet to put the bar up, but today he imagines he's getting up to thirteen, thirteen-six. Nowhere near his PR, but not bad, especially from a five-step. He covers his eyes and squints into the sun as it ebbs below the treeline. It's time to go home. One more, he tells himself, finding his way to the spot on the runway that he's marked by scuffing his shoe in the dirt, his starting point. He lifts the pole, adjusts his grip, and begins his run. *Five-and-four-and-three-and-two-and* . . . He plants, and it's not perfect, a bit to the left, but he's got enough momentum to get a good bend in the pole, to make his body into a backwards *C* before swinging his legs up and getting upside down, then turning over and concaving his chest as he goes over the imaginary bar, and it's only a second, maybe two, that he feels it before he hits the mat, but there it is: complete weightlessness, like flying.

෴

At home he finds Cora on the balcony, watering their potted herbs. It's a beautiful garden, compact and lovely for its useful-ness, and they both take pride in the green blooms of basil and cilantro, rosemary and spindly chives overflowing their containers like hair. Cora has worked hard to keep the plants alive, a difficult task in the muggy Tennessee heat. He'd been surprised when she approached him, four months earlier, about planting a garden; in the six years they'd been married, she'd never shown any inclina-tion toward gardening. It was the idea of nurturing something, of caring for it, that appealed to her, she told him. It was something she thought she was ready to do. He nodded in agreement. It would be much more economical, anyway, he pointed out, to grow herbs at home rather than paying three-fifty a pop at Bi-Lo. She agreed, and then told him that she wanted to have a baby. They planted the garden first; it was a success.

He opens the glass door with some effort, making a mental note to put some WD-40 on the hinges. The condo is old, a rarity in their city, where gargantuan apartment complexes and cookie-cutter subdivisions spring up yearly. In fact, he argued in favor of moving into one such space, pointing out the sleek stainless steel appliances and pool access, but Cora loved the charm of the prewar building, the old telephone nook and the sprawling com-mon rooms outweighing the decades-old dust bunnies under the radiators and the rotted windowsill in the shower.

"Hey, Cor," he says, stepping out onto the balcony. His wife's back is facing him, and he is momentarily grateful for this fact, feeling a flush of shame at his deception of her. "Sorry I'm late, I—"

She waves him off. "It's fine, babe. How was the gym?" She finishes with the pots and hangs the empty watering can on a nail, then turns to smile her lovely smile at him. He feels a pang of sorrow at this thing kept from his wife, and wonders briefly if he should tell her he wasn't lifting weights or hitting the elliptical but that he has been breaking into the high school and pole vaulting, but when he opens his mouth there is no way to explain it, to put into words the feeling of wanting something that is only yours, something secret from the world, something small and good. Instead, he flicks a leaf of basil, which is sturdily and robustly green. "It was good," he says. "How was work?"

Cora works for ETS, developing content for standardized tests: She specializes in math and science questions for the ACT, but also does a bit of work for the GRE. The work is remote, done from wherever she chooses. When she began the job, she often took her laptop to a café downtown by the duck pond, where she'd work until lunch and then stroll the grounds, tossing leftover bits of her sandwich bread to the ducks. Years ago, he'd meet her down there and they'd walk arm-in-arm around the pond, agreeing that they were lucky to live here, that they were happy they decided to stay in the college town where they met, which is affordable and has lovely warm weather for nine months out of the year. Now, more often than not, she stays home all day, only leaving the house for errands or, more rarely, to go for a run. When he questioned her about why she stopped going to the café, she shrugged and said she had tired of their menu, that paying for lunch daily had begun to feel extravagant, especially now that they were saving for a baby. It was a sensible answer, one that shouldn't have been cause for alarm, and yet Ewan sometimes feels concerned about his wife, sheepish in his worry that this turn of events has placed the unfair burden of her happiness on *him*. He works as a claims adjustor for Progressive—not a job with a whole lot of intellectual rigor, but at least it gets him out there, interacting with people. He's arrived at a place of resigned content, surprised to find that he enjoys the rhythm the job gives his life, the regular hours, the nights and weekends it allows him to look forward to.

"Work was work." She is smiling at him, arms wrapped around herself.

"What?" he says.

She shakes her head, lips pursed in a grin. "I was going to wait to tell you," she says.

"What is it?"

She sighs happily. "Ewan"—she pauses significantly—"I think I'm pregnant. I mean, I *know* I am. We're going to have a baby!"

He's seen this moment in his head. He's seen it, too, in movies and television commercials: He's meant to hug Cora with gusto, lift her off the ground and spin her around, before returning her to her feet with particular gentleness, as if just remembering the life in her belly.

Instead he says, "Are you sure? Did you take the test?"

She blushes. "Yes," she says. "It was positive. But I knew before that—I *feel* different. My body, I mean." She puts her hands on her belly.

He smiles, but it feels odd, as if maybe he is baring his teeth at her instead. "I love you so much," he whispers, and they embrace.

ᘓᘇᓍᘔ

He can't sleep. He alternates staring at the ceiling and at the digital clock on his nightstand: *1:00. 2:15. 3:00.* When the clock clicks from 4:59 to 5:00 and he still hasn't fallen asleep, he gets out of bed, pulls on running shorts and grabs his spikes. The roads are empty except for a lone pair of joggers on the sidewalk, moonlight sparking off the reflective strips on their shoes. He's never been an early riser, and it surprises him how much he likes the world like this: quiet, illuminated only briefly and in fragments by the glow of his headlights as he passes. At the track, he hesitates briefly before pulling his car onto the football practice field that is encircled by the track, positioning the headlights to point at the runway. His heart pounds. Technically, he's trespassing: Someone driving by might see the lights and pull over, or call the cops. How would he explain himself? What would he say to Cora if he got a ticket—or arrested?

But he doesn't turn back. Walking from the shed with the poles slung over his shoulder, he looks at the spray of light and thinks that it somehow looks important; like a stage for something much greater, someone more important than him. The air still feels like night and he breathes it in, trying to remember everything about the moment, in case there are no more moments like this. He touches his toes, jogs in place. Takes the runway.

The thing people always want to know about pole vaulting: Have you ever fallen back onto the runway? Ever gotten up to the top without enough momentum and simply come back down, the way you went up? This has always been funny to Ewan: the idea that you'd go up, pause, and then come back down, cartoonishly, delivered to the spot on the runway you'd taken off from. In reality, it was much more likely that you'd stall out mid-vault, lose control of the pole entirely and then come *straight* down, not descending slowly back onto the runway like people imagined but shooting down fast and hard, landing on the front edge of the mat if you were lucky or in the box if you weren't. Pole vaulting is like this: in or out, do or die. This is how he'd explained it to Cora, cocksure in the way that he'd been back then, before things started going south for him as a vaulter. They'd met in astronomy class, which he'd enrolled in with a couple of his buddies, figuring he'd get his Gen Ed science requirement over with the easy way after putting it off for three years, but the class turned out to be tough and his friends had dropped in the second week.

She was a year behind him—a junior—but already well ahead of him in progress toward her degree, which was in education administration with a minor in special literacies. She'd wanted to be a high school principal back then—she'd told him this on their first date, a faux-study session over pizza at Bellacino's, but a few years later had soured on the idea after getting her Master's in education. She was taking the class as an elective—*for fun*, she told him, admitting with a laugh that it was turning out to be harder than she'd counted on. Ewan's major was parks, recreation, and tourism management, more commonly referred to by its initials, PRTM, a major known for its easy classes and popularity among athletes.

"What do you want to do with that?" she asked. She was wearing an oversized sweater that day, with leggings and tan leather cowboy boots; he remembers that because he was sweating in his T-shirt and cargo shorts, thinking that she was probably cooking under all those clothes, but she seemed unbothered.

"With what?"

She laughed at that. "Your major."

"Oh." He shrugged. Even as a senior, it hadn't exactly occurred to him that this was something he needed to begin considering. Graduation seemed ages away—it was only November. He figured he'd have plenty of time to work things out.

"Maybe I'll work at a hotel," he said vaguely. "Or a golf course."

She cocked her head. "You must be quite the pole vaulter."

He grinned. "Why do you say that?"

She smiled, shook her head back and forth in an exaggerated motion, as if to convey that there was something she didn't quite believe about his presence. "Don't know," she said. "But are you?"

He shook his head slowly at her, side to side. Smiled back. "Don't know."

It was three weeks into January before he invited her to watch him vault. The school had already hosted one home meet, a December invitational, but he'd wanted time to shake off the dust from winter break. The ten days he'd spent at home had been drab and bitter-cold, and he'd waited with impatience to get back to what he'd come to think of as his real life. The sun invigorated him, and upon his return he congratulated himself for his decision to attend school down South rather than Michigan, his second choice, where they had an excellent vault coach and good facilities but which was sure to be dreary as hell and where the girls definitely weren't as pretty as they were in Tennessee, where the percentage of the tanned and the blonde seemed incredible to him. Cora wasn't one of these girls—she had dark, fine hair that she kept back in a ponytail and wasn't tan, by southern standards, but had a perpetual pink flush to her cheeks, as if she'd always just returned in a hurry from somewhere pleasurable. Her nose was just-this-side of too long and she had a teeny gap between her front teeth that she told him had been useful for squirting water at playmates as a child. Six weeks into their relationship, Ewan had fallen deeply and irreversibly in love with her.

And so he was happier than he would've probably admitted when he spotted her at the meet, barely in time for the start of the pole vault at three, sipping a hot chocolate from the concessions stand even though the temperature had yet to drop below fifty and they were competing in the indoor facility, anyway. He considered, briefly, jogging around the track to say hello. But it was already ten-till and he was hoping to make his way through the warm-up line for at least one more vault, so he settled for waving to her across the track. He was wearing his singlet, the bright orange-and-white track suit that showed the unambiguous bulge of his package, and wished he still had on his warm-ups: It took the presence of someone from the outside world to make you realize you were clothed fully in spandex. When she waved back, he felt a shock of nervous energy go through him.

Now, when he gets back from the high school, Cora is awake earlier than usual, drinking coffee and using her laptop at the dining room table. Her expression wavers between irritation and concern, as if she is waiting to collect more information before deciding whether or not to be pissed. She asks where he was.

"I couldn't sleep," he says. "I went for a run." He thumbs a callous on his palm and then puts his hands in his pockets.

She frowns. "I heard the car."

He feels himself nodding at this. "I ran stadiums," he says. "I drove over to the university."

There is a brief pause, he thinks, before she nods in response. "Oh." And then: "I should really start working out with you. Would you mind?"

"No." The word catches in his chest, like a hiccup. He clears his throat and smiles at her. "Of course not." He smiles back at her. "You're up early," he says. "Do you want to go get bagels before work?"

⚬◦⚬

The next day, Cora emails him at work with the news that Roland is coming to visit. *Good news! Helen's going to let us borrow R. till Sunday night—she'll drop him off on Friday. Maybe let's go to the park or the univ. museum? Xoxo, Cora.* Roland is Cora's nephew, the eight-year-old son of her older sister. Helen's a single mom, which means that she's always happy for help with her son, somebody to take Roland off her hands for an afternoon or evening. Ewan gets this. He gets, too, that this is a sort of trial run for his own future child. Helen lives eighty miles up 75, an hour's drive, so Roland's visited before, but never without his mom. There have been no overnight visits, much less a whole weekend. But Cora's been leaning on Helen to let them "borrow" Roland—Cora's word—for a weekend, her interest in the boy having increased exponentially since she found out she was pregnant. Ewan understands all of this. And yet he can't help but resent the usurping of his weekend, the fact that it will be spent as a threesome rather than a twosome, that he'll miss out on his three customary Friday night beers, on spending a lazy Saturday morning in bed with his wife. Since Cora got pregnant, he's realized with shamed relief that he's glad that the period of hopeful conceiving is over, that they can go back to having sex for the sake of having sex.

The problem is also that Ewan is terrified of Roland. This is nothing special or accusatory: He's afraid of all children—their smallness, the way they move so quickly, so erratically, like little things belonging in the wild. Often, watching children play, he cringes, imagining their small bones snapping in two. At least, he thinks, Roland has a sensible name, not something pretentious or incongruous or stupid. "DARWIN," he'd once heard a fat, sunburned man yell at his young son, who had dawdled toward the edge of the park that bordered the duck pond and was chasing after the birds, flapping his arms and making loud screeching noises. "Darwin, I *told* you," the man said. "Don't touch them ducks. Them'll *bite* you."

Sounds great!, he types. *There's that new candy store on University—we could go after the park/museum. Kids like candy, right?*

ᐊᔓᐁ

He makes it only two more days before sneaking out to the track after work. The night before, Cora had chattered happily about plans to convert the office into the nursery, about paint colors and furniture and a project involving stencils, and he stayed up late afterwards, unable to sleep, watching re-runs of a National Geographic show about plants that could actually consume small animals.

He tightens the shoelaces on his spikes, his last pair left over from his college gear. It's hot out, the kind of lingering stickiness that in Tennessee lasts well into the evening, and rubs a bit of dirt on his palms to take away the sheen of sweat that has developed on his hands. He picks up one of the poles and heads to the runway, taking four giant steps backward from his dirt-scuff of a starting mark, gets himself ready to do a seven-step approach. It's foolish, estimating the length of his run rather than marking it exactly—pole vaulting is a sport of precision—but he feels greedy, impatient, wanting to do the longer run so that he can vault higher. He lifts the pole, holding it steady at his hip so that it points up and forward, toward the pit. He adjusts his grip, checking for the proper stickiness before beginning his run, counting down to his takeoff. *Seven-and-six-and-five-and-four-and-three-and-two-and . . .*

To this day, he's not sure if it was the fact that Cora was watching him that made him nervous at the meet, or the fact that he was thrown off by the unexpected performance of his teammate, Ricky Hill. Normally, Ricky wouldn't have even competed in the pole vault indoors: He was a decathlete, so he wasn't expected to be good at pole vaulting, just passable. Most decs were good at sprints and hurdles and struggled at the vault, never mastering the technical nuances of the event. Ricky was a big guy—six-five, with long arms that allowed him a better grip height than someone with his level of skill should've been able to pull off—but his technique was horrible, his swing-up premature and his extension more horizontal than vertical. He cleared bars with about as much finesse as Godzilla. Ewan had always felt privately superior to vaulters like Ricky, who raised their grip based on athleticism rather than skill.

And so he was surprised when the meet came down to the two of them: at 4.85 meters, they were the only vaulters who had cleared every height. They had both missed their first two tries at the height. It wasn't an ideal outcome, but Ewan wasn't panicked: If neither of them cleared, Ewan would win on tries—consistency was his greatest strength as a vaulter, and he had cleared every other height on the first attempt.

Still, having Ricky on his heels unsettled him. The two of them watched as the meet volunteers, skinny high school track kids, replaced the crossbar on the standards. Ewan leaned over, pretending to rub out a cramp in his calf muscle.

"Think I can raise it more?" Ricky asked, looking up at the crossbar.

"Raise what?" Ewan rubbed harder.

"My grip. Do you think I can go higher with it? Another handhold? I really think I can get this height. If I can just get—"

"I don't know," Ewan said, bending over his shoes, pretending to tighten the laces. "Probably. Ask Peters." He was growing sulky. "You're flagging off, though," he said as Ricky stood up, brushing black bits of rubber from his hands. "Stay inverted two seconds longer."

When Ricky cleared the height, flinging himself sideways over the crossbar, Ewan tried hard not to feel uncharitable toward his teammate. "Yeah Ricky!" he heard someone call as Ricky pumped two fists in the air and made a show of rolling off the mat.

But still he didn't panic. He still had one attempt, and as long as Ricky didn't clear the next height he'd have a good shot at winning the meet. He *had* to win the meet. Cora was watching and— more important—he was the superior pole vaulter. He *would* clear this height, he told himself, and the next bar, too. He paced back and forth on the side of the runway, pole in hand, practicing the motion of driving his left knee up while extending the pole over his head. His coach, Peters, made a gesture indicating that he should make sure to extend his arms fully at the plant. He nodded.

He took the runway, raising the pole and then lowering it, checking his grip, raising it again. His run felt good, and his timing was spot-on—he left the ground just as the pole slammed into the back of the box—and his swing felt right. He let himself rock back, getting upside down on the pole before turning, releasing . . .

He felt it even before he saw the crossbar come off the standards. His penetration was poor: He hadn't gotten far enough into the pit, the height of his vault occurring six inches in front of the crossbar. It glanced off his shin and he landed on the mat, hard, a fine spray of yellow dust rising from the mat. "Ricky won!" Somebody yelled. Ewan allowed himself to lie there for a moment, eyes closed, not bothering to remove the bar from where it had fallen beneath him.

Now, he lands with a soft *pfff* on his back on the high school's mat, which coughs up a cloud of dust that he'll carefully remove with a lint roller he keeps in his car. It is a good vault, one of the best he's had yet: excellent penetration into the pit, a good vertical release. He rolls off onto the ground and collects his pole.

Four more good vaults and he's ready to call it quits for the day. This is one thing he's noticed about his sessions: He can't get in as many quality jumps as he used to. His body stiffens quicker, his legs refusing to summon the necessary explosive power. Plus, he tells himself, it's ideal to end this way—while you're still in the period of the good, before you get to the bad. This had been the opinion of his high school vault coach, a sixty-something Russian named Plurat, a former All-American in the discus with limited or possibly no previous knowledge of pole vaulting. This was common in public high schools; it was rare to find a school with enough money to hire coaches specifically for each field event. It wasn't uncommon for pole vaulting, so specialized in its technique, to get the shaft.

"Gud to end der," Plurat would say, his smile wide beneath a bristly gray mustache. With his crew-cut and deep-set blue eyes, the old man could've been Bubka's father, had you failed to notice his bird-like ankles and protruding gut, fat carried hard and high up around his heart. "Make for gud movie playing in head." He'd make a swirling motion with his finger near Ewan's temple, and it didn't occur to Ewan until much later, once he was in college and had a young and properly accredited American coach who put in two daily hours on the treadmill and combed his hair into a sharp widow's peak, that Plurat's finger was meant to signify the cranking through of a film reel, the motion of a movie playing on a loop. He'd simply assumed, without ever really thinking about it, that Plurat was making the American hand signal for *crazy*.

ຕຈ*o*ຕ

Roland doesn't want baby carrots for a snack. Roland only eats purple grapes and Cheetos. Roland doesn't like movie theaters and thinks going to the park sounds *stupid*.

Cora, suddenly forced into a half-day of work on Saturday because of a work emergency (she frowned when Ewan asked what exactly constituted a standardized-test-question emergency) has begged him to watch Roland for the morning. "Whatever you want," she said, becoming exasperated when he asked what he was supposed to do with the boy. "Just hang out. Bond with him. It's not rocket science."

He's finding that she was right: It isn't rocket science. Because rocket science would make sense, would have the ability to be expressed in algorithms and formulas. Rocket science would not stare blankly at the punch line of his jokes, and then say "Ha. Ha.," in a voice covered in sarcasm before returning its full attention to its cell phone.

"How about the batting cages? What if we go hit some pitches?" The two of them are in Ewan's car, looping around the city after his suggestions of the park, the movies, and the bike-rental shop, in that order, were summarily rejected.

Roland shrugs. The boy, bustling with energy when Helen dropped him off the evening before, has gone practically catatonic. They pull up to a red light.

"Hey, Roland," Ewan tries again. He is getting desperate. "What if we stopped by my work—I could show you around while nobody's there? Does that sound fun?" He turns to face Roland, considers winking at him before chickening out at the last moment.

Roland looks up from his phone with dead eyes. "No," he says, and sneezes in the direction of Ewan's face.

"Helen says he's just that way with men," Cora whispered to him in the kitchen that morning. "He hasn't, you know, had the best experience with them. Don't take it personally." And so Ewan has driven the same figure-eight route around town three times trying not to take it personally, both of them looking at the clock to see when they could be released from captivity and returned to Cora.

But! There is hope: Roland showed signs of life when Ewan mentioned pole vaulting.

"What is that?" he'd said, still suspicious, eyes still on his phone's screen.

"It's where you get a really long pole," Ewan said, "and you run as fast as you can and then jump, and the pole lifts you up high over a bar, and then you fall onto a mat. It's superfun." He hears his voice take on a corny animation, an annoying over-eagerness. He has never before used the word *superfun*.

"Sounds cool," Roland said carefully.

"It is cool. It's extremely cool."

And so they have ended up at the high school track, where Ewan thanked God or some higher power that it was the fall and not the spring, which would mean track season and the track being in use for a home meet or the poles traveling on the bus (they'd put them on the floor under the seats, where they'd roll back and forth, knocking against the kids' feet) to an away meet.

At the shed, Roland wants to know why Ewan has to dig the key out from under the mat. "Why don't you just keep it? You could put it in your keychain." Ewan's keychain is the only other thing he has been able to get Roland interested in: It has a tiny replica of a Corona bottle with a small light that blinks yellow when touched. He hopes, without really caring, that

Helen won't be angry at him for letting Roland play with beer-related paraphernalia.

"Uh," Ewan says. "It's just easier this way." Roland seems unsatisfied with this, and he gropes for a better lie. "It's so the other, uh, coaches who need to use the shed can use the key, too." He cringes inwardly at the bad quality of the lie. "That way we *share* the key." He looks at Roland significantly at the word *share*.

Roland shows no signs of recognition at the word—*Helen's fault*, Ewan thinks automatically, before immediately rolling back the thought and trying to cover it up with more generous ones. *Helen is a single mother. Helen does her best. Sharing is overrated.*

Roland doesn't press him about the key anymore, and Ewan opens the shed.

"Stay out there," he says, trying to imitate the stern authority he has heard in other parents' voices.

"Why?"

He pauses. It's a fair question. "Okay, come in," he says.

He enlists Roland's help in finding the smallest pole in the shed. It turns out to be a purple-and-white striped women's pole, a Big Stick, only ten feet long. He recalls a teeny freshman vaulter, Tina Marie, from his last year coaching, and wonders if they bought the pole specifically for her after he left; normally, eleven feet would be the minimum length for a women's pole, even in high school. The flex rating is 110 pounds; which has got to be way more than Roland weighs, and anyway the boy isn't going to be putting any kind of bend in the pole. He hands it to Roland and tells him to carry it over to the runway. He guesses that the boy, who is tall for his age, isn't much shorter than Tina Marie was, though he's certainly thinner and probably less coordinated. He shakes his head at the thought. What, exactly, is he planning to do with Roland? Teach him drills? Show him how to properly lower the pole into the pit, in slow motion? Let him actually *vault*? He has no plan. He tells himself that he won't take any jumps, but grabs a couple of men's poles from the shed, just in case, and jogs out.

Roland is actually not a bad pole vaulter. After doing a half-hour of drills, Ewan feels the boy growing impatient and decides to actually let him get on the runway, figuring there's no way for Roland to harm himself without getting very far off the ground. Ewan has him holding low on the pole, so he isn't getting much height—new vaulters never do, anyway, not during their first session—but Roland's take-off seems to have some power, and he's clutching the pole in a wily, determined way, flinging himself onto the mat fearlessly. Ewan finds himself getting excited over the boy's progress, clapping and shouting foolishly, running alongside Roland as he trots down the runway, and it's kind of nice, too, that when he explains the mechanics of the vault Roland isn't old enough to giggle at the word *penetration* the way the high-schoolers always did. It is unlikely that Roland understands *penetration*—or *sailpiece*, for that matter—but Roland refuses to dumb his explanation down, standing firm in a belief that he should treat children like adults, a belief he heard somewhere he can't remember now and which made good sense at the time.

"Roland, yes!" He claps his hands as the boy propels himself onto the mat, landing properly on his back like Ewan taught him. He waits for him to scramble off the mat before clamping his hand on Roland's shoulder. "Want to stop on that one? It's always good to end on a good vault—that's what my old coach taught me." Roland is grinning at him, and Ewan notices for the first time that the boy has the same tiny gap between his teeth that Cora has.

"No!" Roland shouts, jumping up and down. "No! No! No! I want to do it more!"

Ewan shrugs. "Your call, bud."

Forty minutes after watching Ricky win the meet, Ewan sought out Cora, finding her watching the triple jump with polite interest from the stands. He knew he should've come to her sooner, that he shouldn't have lingered in the men's room, sitting on top of the closed toilet, pouting, but even as he knew these things he hadn't been able to stop himself from doing them.

"That was amazing!" she said, rising to hug him. "You came in second, right?"

"Yeah," he scoffed. "Second."

"Second's good," she said. She had caught the sharpness in his voice, and the statement came out like a question.

"Second sucks," he said, and kicked the aluminum beneath them with the toe of his shoe. He hadn't bothered to change out of his spikes or put his warm-ups on over his singlet. "*Ricky* sucks." He knew he was being an asshole. But he couldn't bring himself to make a joke about it, to self-deprecate, to smile at her and say he'd do better next time. He'd always been a sore loser. It occurred to him that it had been a stupid move to invite her to the meet, that there'd been a good chance of exposing this side of himself to her. But he hadn't anticipated this outcome, this mood. He'd anticipated winning. He'd anticipated an excellent mood.

"You did really well, too," Cora tried. "Your last attempt was so close . . ."

"He's not supposed to beat me," Ewan exhaled, more frustration in his voice than he'd planned on. "He's a *decathlete*, for Chrissake. His technique is *horrible*."

He turns his attention back to Roland, who wants to know why Ewan isn't pole vaulting: Isn't he any *good* at it? After two hours—a marathon vault session—Roland has showed no signs of slowing down, and Ewan is starting to get annoyed. Annoyed that the boy doesn't seem to understand the context of his compliments, that Roland is doing well for his first time on the runway, yeah, but *he still sucks*. Annoyed that when he turns his back

Roland pokes him in the asscheek with his pole, giggling wildly. Annoyed that he has begun to taunt Ewan about his own vaulting. Finally, he gives in. "You want to see me vault?" Roland nods up and down in a fast, exaggerated motion. "Yeah!"

"Okay," he says. "I'll vault."

He doesn't even bother with warm-ups—he's already limbered up from running alongside the boy and pushing him up onto the mat—just grabs a pole and finds his mark on the runway.

"Here goes nothing," he says out loud, to nobody. Standing on the runway with Roland watching, Ewan thinks about what a dick he was back then, how arrogant in his own self-righteous anger, how he should have been surprised that Cora stayed with him but wasn't. *Second sucks.*

He cocks the pole up and runs. It's a better-than-average vault, especially done without warm-up, and Roland claps wildly as he lands gracefully on the mat.

"That was *awesome*," he yells, jumping onto the mat where Ewan lies. Ewan holds up his hand for a high-five, feels the slap of a small palm against his.

And so they begin trading off vaults, the boy watching and clapping as Ewan raises his grip, getting good power in his jumps. But it isn't long before his annoyance returns. Soon, Roland is less than impressed with his own vaulting, wants to *go higher*— his words—wants to put the bar up, begins resisting when Ewan tries to pull him off the runway for refresher drills when his technique goes too far awry, his arms bent and his legs windmilling like crazy. It is, in Ewan's mind, the worst outcome for a vaulter: the abandonment of technique in favor of immediate results, the reliance on athleticism and speed to get yourself over the bar. No child of *his* would be allowed to vault this way.

"You *will* go higher," Ewan explains, "if you get the movements down."

Roland makes a sound like a growl and crosses his arms over his chest.

Ewan tries again. "Look," he says. "Begin with the pole at your hip, like we talked about, right? Then bring it up to your ear before extending it over your head. The pole should always stay close to your body. Right?"

Roland makes a fart noise with his mouth. He rolls his eyes. Even though he shouldn't be—Roland's just a kid, after all—Ewan is taken aback by this, by the boy's sudden slide backward in progress and in attitude.

"Fine," he says. "You want me to put the bar up?"

Roland brightens. "Yeah!"

"Okay," he says. "Let's put the bar up."

He places the bar carefully on the standards, where it is approximately even with the height of his own neck. "Okay," he says. "Find your mark on the runway. Count your steps as you run—remember? Lower your pole on three, jump on one."

"*Okay.*" Roland is exasperated; they have been over this before.

His first vault with a crossbar is a disaster, a flailing and splaying of limbs across the mat. Roland's take-off is all wrong: He's bending his arms when he plants, hugging the pole to himself rather than pushing it out.

"Okay," Ewan says. He can feel the heat returning to his face: This is wrong, all wrong. "All right. That's good for your first try, but now we should talk about a few things, maybe run through a couple more drills to really get the motions cemented in your head."

Roland's face darkens. "This *sucks*," he says. "I don't want to do any more drills. Drills are *boring*. I want to go *higher*."

Ewan feels a ball of dread tightening in his chest. Dread at Roland's stalled progress. Dread at bringing this ungrateful little goblin to the track, *his* track—for what?

"Well," Ewan can feel his face flush hot out of anger, "if you want to go higher, you have to raise your grip on the pole. To raise your grip on the pole, you have to have good technique."

Roland's face relaxes as he considers this. "Can't I just raise my grip instead?"

"No."

"Why not?"

"Because you're not ready. You need to do more drills."

"I don't WANT TO DO MORE DRILLS!" Roland's voice rises into a crescendo. Ewan puts his hands up.

"FINE," he yells back. "DON'T DO MORE DRILLS."

"OKAY."

Ewan grabs his pole and takes the runway. His run is good, the rhythm of his feet slapping the runway exactly right, and he raises his arms with the pole overhead, feeling the pushback as it slams into the back of the box, the momentum pushing against him strong but his body stronger, and he feels himself lift high into the air. He releases the pole at the apex of his vault, and at that moment, Roland isn't there—*nothing* is there; nothing exists—and he savors the feeling, savors those two seconds of time away from the world. And then feels his body land on the mat.

When he rolls back onto his feet, he squints at a figure taking a seat on the far side of the bleachers.

"Is that *Cora*?" he says aloud, not to Roland so much as himself.

"*Aunt* Cora," Roland corrects.

He reaches to brush the yellow dust from his clothes, automatically, as if this will be the thing that saves him, that preserves his secret.

"What is she doing here?" he says. Cora waves.

"She *texted* me," Roland says, as if this is the most obvious explanation in the world. "She asked if we were having fun. I said we were pole vaulting."

Ewan feels the dread again, greater this time, and he's angry, too, pissed at Roland for giving him away—and at himself for thinking that the boy wouldn't.

"Wait here," he says.

"Hey," he says, jogging up to her, waiting for her to say more before he does, trying to get a read on her reaction. Trying to figure out his *own* reaction—or his story, at least. He doesn't have to confess the secret vaulting sessions: He could say that he brought Roland to the high school and taught him to vault, only taking a couple of vaults himself; she wouldn't know that it had taken him ten weeks to get back to where he was, wouldn't be able to distinguish a thirteen-and-a-half foot jump from a fourteen-and-a-half one, *she* isn't a pole vaulter, after all . . .

"Hey."

He gestures toward Roland. "He texted you?"

She nods. "He said you guys were pole vaulting. I was going to drive over to the other high school if I didn't find you here." She hesitates. "When he said *pole vaulting*, I didn't think that *you* . . ."

And it all spills out. The vaulting sessions for the last ten weeks, the car pulled onto the football field, the lies about the gym. With his confession comes no relief, only a deep sorrow that it is over, that she's seen him pole vault, surely seen the pure pleasure he takes in the act, this thing he has held onto so fiercely as his own. Stupidly, he brought Roland into it—and now Cora, too. She has seen it and now it is ruined. "I'm sorry," he says flatly.

"I'm afraid of having a baby, too, you know." Her voice trembles. "We're bringing a person into the world—it's *terrifying*."

In college, Sergey Bubka became Ewan's personal hero. It was an obvious choice, sure, like a basketball player idolizing Jordan—Bubka had set and reset his own world records with virtually no competition for almost a decade—but it was the man's cool determination in the sport, his six-meter jump when people thought it couldn't be done, his 6.14m clearance in '94 that set a new world record after commentators began predicting the beginning of his decline in the sport. Ewan thinks now about the first time Cora visited his apartment, how she giggled at the Bubka poster taped up in the kitchen, and even though the resentment is years old, has disintegrated and fallen to pieces with the passing of time, he feels the tinge of it return now, the flavor of it odious and repugnant as rust.

"That's not—" he begins, but Cora isn't looking at him, is looking away, down at the runway, where Roland is raising his pole.

"Is it okay," she says, "for him to be doing that?"

Ewan glances over. "It's fine." But he sees, just as the boy begins his run, that Roland has raised his grip six inches from where Ewan has told him to hold. It's much too high; there's no way that Roland will get enough momentum to clear the bar, much less make it into the pit. At best, he'll knock the bar down. At worst . . .

Ewan should call to him. Make him stop. Insist on more drills, or call it quits for the day. But a small, dark part of him wants to allow Roland the jump. Wants him to knock the bar down. Wants him to see that he's wrong and Ewan's right: that technical mastery always trumps athleticism. Wants to be able to tell himself that he and Roland are nothing alike, that his own joy in the act of pole vaulting is unsullied by impatience, by greed for results.

Roland plants the pole and jumps. Ewan can see that it's bad: The pole actually gives a tiny bend and Roland is yanked under it before he even has a chance to begin his swing, the pole giving a reverse-release and flinging him to the ground. He lands awkwardly in the box, limbs splayed everywhere, elbow pointing down and legs sticking up.

"Ow!" he cries, his small voice echoing up to where they sit. Cora has already stood up and is going to him, running in the awkward gait of a person in street clothes, legs restricted by denim and sandals clutched to feet by toes. Ewan follows, purposely hanging a step behind.

"Why did you *let him?*" Cora says as she runs to the boy, not waiting for an answer but going to where Roland sits on the runway. Roland is holding his arm, rubbing his elbow, and Ewan can see from where he stands that the boy is probably okay; probably just bruised, he's moving his arm and it's extending normally; there are no protruding bones. He has stopped crying and is looking at Ewan with a deadly and accusatory stare. Ewan moves closer, touches his wife's shoulder. "Cora," he says softly. Her shoulder shifts from beneath his hand.

He steps back slowly, moves away. No one notices.

He watches Cora tending to the boy, wiping a tear from beneath Roland's eye with her thumb and then holding out his elbow to examine, the two of them like a little family apart from the world. He has the feeling of being much further from them than he actually is, feeling that if he were to call to them his voice would disappear before reaching them, his words moving away from them in rings, and it is then that he feels the adrenaline of fear slip away and in its place a weight like lead in his belly, the dread and gloom and terror over spoiling something pure and good and right.

The Second Wife

The first wife was dead, which called for a reverence of spirit when speaking of her, a lowered voice and furrowed, sympathetic brow, but the problem was that the second wife didn't feel reverent. She felt fascinated, curious—but not reverent. She liked to ask questions about her, questions like which sections of the newspaper had she enjoyed most and did she always cook a vegetable side dish with dinner (the second wife did not) and what were her thoughts on movies in which a man and a woman switched bodies? There was a gingerliness embedded in the husband's manner as he answered these questions. The second wife sensed that he felt they were disrespectful of the first wife's memory, but she did not. When I die, she often said, I hope there is someone who wants to know if I liked eating cantaloupe in the summer and going to amusement parks.

She liked cantaloupe fine, the husband would sigh, or We never went to an amusement park together, and the second wife would record these tidbits in her mind, like a court reporter. She also began revealing her own views and estimations to the husband. She tried to make these strong, interested opinions, so that in case she died he would have better information to report to the third wife; he could do more than sigh and say I don't know. He would know, for example, that she liked black beans but not pinto, would be able to report that she found the idea of eating fish on Fridays appealing, though she hadn't been raised Catholic.

There were still signs of the first wife around the house. Her charcoal sketches of farmhouses and barns hung in the dining room, and her golfing trophies stood tall and proud on a shelf in the study. When the second wife wondered aloud at the first wife's natural athletic prowess, the husband glanced at the trophies and remarked that they should be moved to the basement.

There was a small black dog, the first wife's dog, and the second wife often held him on her lap as she watched TV, thinking This is the dog that my husband's dead wife petted, or I wonder if he likes me as much as he liked her. He (the dog) appeared to like her (the second wife) a good deal, settling in against her thigh when she sat down on the couch. He seemed to enjoy the same television programs she did.

At some point the second wife began wearing the first wife's clothes. They hung neatly in the guest room closet: The husband had not bothered to get rid of them. The second wife began to feel sorry for them, and asked the husband wouldn't he please take them to Goodwill or the Salvation Army so that they might be *worn* again, these poor clothes, hanging there so hopefully. When he refused, she began to wear them—slowly at first, just scarves and socks, until it became clear that the husband wasn't going to notice. It made the clothes happier, she told herself, and anyway the first wife was much more fashionable than the second wife had ever been.

And so it wasn't long until she was going through the first wife's clothes with abandon, reveling in this new sartorial world that had been so quickly and so gloriously opened to her, putting on the first wife's bomber jackets and pencil skirts and ankle boots and admiring herself in the mirror. She would wear these things out to coffee shops, or the grocery store, all the time thinking, This is the cardigan that a dead woman wore, or This hat was on the head of my husband's late wife. She couldn't get over the novelty of it. It was like knowing a celebrity.

When she discovered the first wife's collection of cookbooks, stashed inconveniently in one of the lower cabinets, behind the immersion blender and other seldom-used small appliances, her heart fluttered. These were well-worn, frequently used cookbooks, with the pages of favorite recipes dog-eared and lovely little notes written in the margins, phrases like *good with rice!* and *less butter okay* (¼ c.)

She sat the husband down and spoke to him with great seriousness. Why was he hiding these? The first wife was a part of him and she (the second wife) wanted her (the first wife) to be a part of her, too. Besides, didn't he miss eating his favorite meals?

I didn't know you liked to cook, the husband said. To be frank, I wasn't aware that you knew *how* to cook. He gestured at the refrigerator, where she had pinned a magnet shaped like a take-out menu, holding five or six actual take-out menus. She had always thought this rather clever.

She softened. I *don't*, she said. Know how. But I'm going to learn.

That night, she felt it almost a blasphemy that she ruined the eggplant parmesan that the first wife had so painstakingly notated. She hadn't let the eggplant weep enough—either that or it had wept too much or too passionately; whatever it was, it had worked itself into quite a soggy mess.

I'm awful, she said, flinging down the casserole dish before the husband. I can't even duplicate a simple recipe.

The husband was cutting into the eggplant parmesan with a spatula. It seemed that, in addition to being overly watery, it was also very tough, and he had to stand up to get more leverage.

Did she make this often? The second wife asked.

The husband shrugged. Every now and then. He put a wet, messy serving of eggplant on her plate. It reminded the second wife generally, though not precisely, of brains.

What was it like when she made it? The second wife persisted. Was it like this? Of course it wasn't like this. She was meticulous. Right? Wasn't she meticulous?

The husband chewed a piece of eggplant for a long time. Do you want to know what she was like? He said finally. I can tell you what she was like.

Oh, yes. Thank you.

The husband put down his fork. She was confident to the point of arrogance, he said. But she was insecure, too: If she sensed that you were less than overjoyed about eating the dinner she'd planned, she'd refuse to make it, and she'd make you choose something else instead, like pizza. At first you'd refuse and say you wanted her food but she'd press hard and finally you'd give in and get the pizza and then she'd take this as proof that you really didn't want to eat her cooking and be pissed at you. And then when you did eat her food, it didn't taste good.

The second wife frowned. Go on, she said.

She performed these complicated moral calculations in order to determine if things were fair, the husband said. If we saw her parents for three days at Thanksgiving, we saw mine for no more than three at Christmas, even though we both had more days off of work then.

She was very . . . *precise*, okay. Detail-oriented, I'd say. But generous, too. I bet she gave great Christmas gifts.

They were okay. I think last year she got me a gift certificate.

To where?

I don't remember. Does it matter?

If it was for somewhere you really like, it might have been a great gift.

It wasn't.

So she was frugal about gifts, the second wife said. But you were kidding about the food, right? She was a good cook. Better than this. The second wife held up a forkful of eggplant, a string of cheese hanging from fork to plate.

The husband considered this, and then took another bite. No, he said. This is actually an improvement.

CHAPTER

Soon after that the second wife began sleeping in, getting out of bed later and later each day until finally she was not getting out of bed at all, except sometimes at night, to eat ice cream right out of the box, or to get her laptop to order more of the mystery novels that she liked.

I think I'm sick, she called one night into the living room, where the husband was watching a movie.

Hmmm? The husband said. Do you want me to get you something? I can go to the drug store.

No, she said. I think it's bad. I think it might be . . . something very bad.

She heard the husband get up from the couch in the living room, and then she heard the jangle of the dog's collar as he, too, rose. He had taken to sitting next to the husband, not her, as if exasperated by her sleeping habits.

The husband came in and stroked her forehead, pushing back her bangs, which she had purposefully not washed for two or three days—but not longer, because that would be gross.

There's a tea I used to make for her when she was sick, the husband said. I could make you some.

The second wife brightened. Would you?

And so they continued on like this: He made tea for her in the morning before he left for work, a second cup when he returned. He sat on the bed while she drank it, and she used this time to tell him all about herself, in case she died, about how her mother believed that you shouldn't mix too many food groups in the same meal and why she disliked the man her sister had married and how she got the scar on her elbow (a game of Red Rover, age nine). He nodded politely, but she wasn't convinced, and took to keeping a diary, but soon many of the words in the sentences she wrote down seemed extraneous, and she began just writing lists: *All-Time Favorite Songs* and *Five Dream Vacation Destinations*. Sometimes there were short paragraphs, mini-dissertations on specific matters, like *Thoughts on Five Varieties of Poker*, or sometimes just singularly titled subjects, like *Toucans*. She kept her notes in a leather-bound journal that she found to be very beautiful. The journal had belonged to the first wife, though she had never written in it except to record her name and phone number on the inner cover, in case the book were to become lost. The second wife often stared at the individual digits, running her fingers over them and thinking that surely the husband was wrong about the first wife.

A doctor came and went. There's nothing wrong with you, he said, and the second wife thought him most unsympathetic because she knew he'd been paid extra to make a house call; he could have at least diagnosed her with anxiety, or allergies. She would write a paragraph about him, she decided, in the first wife's leather-bound journal, and when she touched the beautiful soft leather of its cover, she felt that she could not possibly continue on this way, that she would get her own journal, not leather-bound but made of some other fine material, one that was beautiful and unexpected and fashioned from something that eclipsed leather, like feathers. But as she lifted her tea—the first wife's tea—from the nightstand to take a sip, as she turned to the next blank page and wrote *The Doctor*, she thought to herself that perhaps she wouldn't get her own journal, that she'd better press forward with this one instead. And though the tea had grown cold, the taste of it on her tongue remained the same, a taste that was rich and sweet, and it nourished her to the core.

Velvet Canyon

The announcement about the bathroom is worrisome. Lane had not before considered the logistics of the bathroom, which are: You will poop in a bucket. They are also to pee in a bucket, albeit a separate one that will later be dumped into the river. What will happen to the poop is unclear.

Lane glances toward her daughter, Mandy, whose gaze is resolutely neutral. The trip is only thirty-six hours long; perhaps pooping can be avoided altogether.

At any rate, one must press onward: Lane is here to eat a hallucinogenic cactus and a hallucinogenic cactus she will eat. She turns her attention intently to their drug administrator/camping guide, Lorenzo, as he explains the sequence of events for the trip, which basically go: hike into canyon, set up camp, sleep. Wake up, hike to special, secret part of canyon, do drugs. Wait for drugs to wear off, hike back, go home. "Light meals will be provided," he adds. She nods along. Lorenzo is tall and hulking, with a cloud of orange hair and a matching beard, a film of hairy curls on his arms and legs. He looks timeless and mythical, like a Norse god, a leader of men.

They are standing at the trailhead to Velvet Canyon in Arizona, where Canyon Excursions has been dealing in casual drug tourism since 2003. The canyon is a small, relatively unknown dip in the earth tucked near the southern end of the Mogollon Rim. At the bottom, Lorenzo tells them, there is a river: a tiny, tricking offshoot off the Hassayampa Basin. The place is called Velvet Canyon for the purple algae covering the rocks that line the river. "It has been suggested that the algae is mildly toxic to mammals," Lorenzo says. "Which is why you won't see a lot of other people down there." He winks, quickly, a barely perceptible flashing of the eyelid. A quiet giggle escapes a few of the campers.

An old woman with very thin legs raises her hand. "Will the toxic algae interfere with the hallucinogenic effects of the cactus?" she asks.

"Good question," Lorenzo says. "Very good question. The short answer is: no. The longer answer is: We're not entirely sure. But I can assure you that the experience will be highly satisfactory. In customer surveys the San Pedro Cactus has an approval rating of over eighty-five percent for first-time users."

The group nods eagerly. They are all women: pairs of friends, mostly, maybe a lesbian couple or two. Most of them are elderly, a decade or so older than Lane herself. She is pretty sure that earlier she heard the thin-legged woman actually introduce herself to someone as *Gladys.*

"First things first, though," Lorenzo says. "There's something we like to do before anything else. Something to help you get to know each other before we embark on this *journey.* I think you'll like it. It's a tradition, kind of."

Lane feels a flutter of excitement: What will this, their first drug-related ritual, be? She already feels a warmth toward these women, with their springy gray hairstyles and their high-tech water bottles and their extra-thick wool socks, folded over once, carefully, at the ankle. She leans in.

"The Name Game." Lorenzo beams. "Best icebreaker there is. Circle up. Go on, get in tight. Nobody bites. Well, ha, except for maybe Allison."

The women form a circle, chuckling politely. They are in circumstances for which the correct social etiquette has not yet been defined. How do you treat the people with whom you will soon commit an illegal, if victimless, act? They sit down, kindergarten-style, on a large afghan Lorenzo has spread out. It's mid-afternoon, the Arizona sun hot and high. Lane dabs at her forehead with a sweat-wicking handkerchief purchased specifically for the trip. She isn't sweating much. The desert is like that.

"Okay," Lorenzo says. "Here's how it works. I say, *I'm Lorenzo, and I'm bringing lima beans.* The alliteration helps the memory, get it? Repeat the names and then add your own, plus an item you'd bring to an imaginary picnic, or camping trip, or what have you." He adds, by way of explanation: "Before I did this, I used to teach fifth grade."

"You start." He nods at the woman next to Gladys.

"I'm Betty, and I'm bringing"—she gulps nervously, an inhale of a giggle—"bread? Is that okay?" Except for Mandy, who stands with her arms crossed, disapproval wafting from her like someone's excess cologne, they are all giddy, happy with anticipation. For most of them, it will be their first experience with illegal drugs.

"Okay, Betty is bringing bread," Lorenzo says. "Good. Next."

"She's Betty and she's bringing bread. I'm Gladys, and I'm bringing, ah, *gherkins.*" Gladys looks pleased with herself.

"Gladys with the gherkins. Very good. This will be a quick group, I can tell already."

The repetitions pick up speed, voices joyously calling out names and their matching ingredients, all of them tittering when Allison, who is gruff and large, announces she will bring *alligator meat.* When they get to Mandy, who excelled at memorization exercises in grade school, she repeats the ten names before her own flawlessly.

"Mandy, mayo," she says in a bored voice.

"Mandy Mayo," Lorenzo repeats. "Like a superhero of sandwiches. Okay, Mandy Mayo, nicely done."

He turns to Lane. She is the last one. "She's Betty and she's bringing bread," Lane begins, her voice wobbly and uncertain; will she be able to remember all of the names, all the picnic items? But she gains strength with each name that she speaks aloud, feeling a growing camaraderie with this group of women who have, like her, come to the desert to have an adventure, and when she has finished listing the names of the eleven women who came before her, her voice rings out loud and clear as she announces that she will be bringing licorice, and that there's plenty to go around.

꩜

The decision to eat a hallucinogenic cactus at the bottom of an Arizona canyon had happened like this: Lane, having very little experience with drugs—if you don't count copious amounts of caffeine, ha ha ha—had found herself divorced six months earlier, suddenly freed not only from a cautious and disapproving husband but also from any restraints on her behavior. She could do literally anything she wanted. She could climb a volcano in Ecuador! Visit a male gigolo in Hong Kong! What would she do! In the end, she'd booked a slot on a guided two-day drug excursion through a shady internet company she learned about from one of her regular passengers, an aging hippie type who sometimes discreetly tried to sell marijuana to the other passengers on the Las Vegas shuttle bus she drove for a living. His name was Stu. He'd recommended the San Pedro Cactus out of a short list of overnight excursions for people wanting to warm up to drugs in a safe-yet-scenic outdoor location. There was a women-only option, and Lane chose it, in a hasty attempt to—to what? To avoid men, she thought, but maybe also: to avoid happily married couples, puffing (harmoniously) or injecting each other (devotedly) or whatever it was one did to ingest the San Pedro Cactus;

she wasn't quite clear on that. *Perfect for beginners*, Stu had said approvingly. *Plus, you can tell your family you're going hiking.*

And so Lane told Mandy, her thirty-eight-year-old daughter, that she was going hiking. This turned out to be a mistake: Mandy had shown up at Lane's house that morning and announced she was coming along. "Girl trip," she'd said, and tossed her overstuffed duffel bag into Lane's trunk. Mandy had a proclivity for the Misplaced Grand Gesture: She'd once driven eight hours home from college to celebrate her parents' anniversary with them. The table for two at Piero's had suddenly felt very crowded indeed.

"You have to be signed up," Lane had said weakly, a faint panic pitter-pattering in her heart. Mandy, a fastidious rule-abider who had worn a *Crack is Whack!* pin on her backpack as a teenager, would definitely not approve of the trip's more nefarious purposes.

Mandy shrugged her off. "What's one more person?" she said. "If there aren't extra tents, I'll squeeze in with you. I don't mind."

"But—"

"Mom." Mandy arched an eyebrow. "Come on. We never spend time together."

It was true: Mandy herself had recently become single, and Lane had shied away from spending time with her daughter in the midst of her breakup. She hadn't wanted to hear Mandy's rationalizations about Jad, whom she'd never liked.

"How about next weekend?" Lane said. "We'll go to the spa. Or the movies!"

"Mom, no. Sorry, but I'm coming with."

Panic morphed into irritation, and it occurred to Lane that she might use the opportunity to teach Mandy a lesson. Mandy was square as a box. Mandy wouldn't want to do drugs. Let Mandy come along! Mandy would have a bad time. Mandy would learn something about butting in on other people's plans. It didn't feel good, wanting to exact this small revenge on her daughter, except it sort of did.

"Okay," she said. "Let's go."

She helped Mandy load her sleeping bag and her hiking boots and her gallon-sized Ziploc full of dehydrated mixed fruit into the trunk, and off they went.

The four-hour trip felt much longer than it really was.

Mandy said: "I think what I was feeling the whole time was that Jad and I were so much alike, so *on the same level*, that it got kind of intense, being in each other's heads like that. Can two souls be *too* kindred? I don't know, I guess is what I'm saying." She munched thoughtfully on an apricot. "Cynthia says it's okay to acknowledge feelings of pain and regret."

Cynthia was one of Mandy's friends, who had done a semester of psychology in college.

Lane herself didn't feel much pain over the dissolution of her marriage, and even less regret. She and Mandy's father, Lonnie, had split up over submarine sandwiches that February, her having had the sudden but certain realization that she no longer wanted to be married. She can still remember the shock on Lonnie's face when she told him: He'd been mid-bite into his meatball sub, and his face had gone frozen with a swath of marinara at the corner of his mouth, red and viscous as blood. She'd reached over and dabbed it with a napkin, her last tender marital action toward him.

Mandy, on the other hand, had been dating Jad for only a handful of months—and Lane suspected he'd hung around that long only for the free rent. She'd met him a couple of times early on, once when he'd suggested dinner for three at a fancy seafood restaurant, where he'd ordered a twenty-four-dollar lobster pot pie and then, in the manner of a highly magnanimous person, leaned back and allowed Lane to pay the bill. When he'd disappeared for good, Lane's heart had ached for her daughter—a little—but the ache had been covered up by a more powerful relief.

Mandy talked about Jad through Nevada and into Arizona, past the Joshua Trees and into the Mojave Desert. An hour from the trailhead, after a brief interlude on a documentary she'd seen about people who lived in very very small houses, she talked about Jad some more: "He was *so* kind to animals," she said.

Annoyance had bubbled up in Lane's gut like indigestion. She'd looked forward to making the four-hour drive on her own, the sky spread out over the highway, engine whirring and tires trembling a bit as she topped the car out at eighty, eighty-five, just enough to feel a little bit *fast.* She'd rolled the name of the place, *Velvet Canyon,* around in her mouth like something good to eat. She'd happily anticipated getting away from the Strip, from the siren song of the bright video poker machines, where despite knowing better she played hand after hand at the Super Double Double Bonus 5 too conservatively to ever win more than a few bucks—and lost more often. She tried to muster sympathy for her daughter but came up empty.

"If I were the betting kind," Mandy said, "I'd bet we'll be back together within the month, as soon as he's not under so much pressure at work." Jad was in sales at a company that manufactured parts for industrial-sized blenders and other kitchen equipment.

Something rushed forth in Lane like hot steam released from a valve. In a very calm voice, she said: "Mandy, the purpose of this trip is to eat a San Pedro Cactus in order to hallucinate."

Mandy's mouth, which had begun talking about Jad's undiagnosed personality disorder, stopped moving around whatever word it was about to form.

"There's hiking, too," Lane added. "But the cactus is the, uh, the *main attraction.*" She cleared her throat. "I'm an adult, and I have decided I'd like to try hallucinating, just this once. You are welcome to join me." Her voice sounded oddly formal.

Mandy's lower lip hung down lazily in the way it used to do when she was a teenager. It was a facial quirk Lane had always hoped she'd outgrow.

"You're kidding, right?" she said after a moment. "This is all some kind of totally fucked joke, right? Excuse my French." As a child, Mandy had taken a gleeful joy in admonishing her mother for her occasional swearing.

"No joke." Lane kept her gaze straight ahead. "You don't have to come with me," she said after a moment. "I can drop you at the bus station in Prescott."

"And then what?"

"And then you can go home. I guess."

Mandy shook her head. "No," she said. "If you're going, I'm going. No offense, but it's starting to look like this divorce has thrown you off the deep end."

◌◦◦◦◌

At the bottom of Velvet Canyon, dusk has fallen. After the Name Game, the four-mile hike had taken longer than expected: There was a lot of gear to carry—tents and camp chairs and sleeping bags—and the group was fit but elderly, moving at a steady, plodding pace. They'd taken a couple of hours after that to set up camp and eat a simple dinner of rice and beans.

Mandy had been mostly quiet on the hike, hanging toward the back of the pack, though once she'd hurried up beside Lane to announce, in a breathless whisper, that she was pretty sure the whole thing was a scam. "Yeah," she said. "I remember hearing about it on NPR. They convince a bunch of people they're getting something expensive, like drugs, and then they take their money and don't show up."

"But—we're already on the trip," Lane said. "So it doesn't really make sense."

"Right," Mandy said. "That's how they get you."

Lane gestured at Lorenzo, *Canyon Excursions* embroidered officially on his tank top. "Not a scam," she had whispered.

Thankfully, Mandy has mostly dropped it, sulking quietly but at least in the company of the others, all of them sitting around a fire that Lorenzo has lit with a starter log made of something other than actual wood. "Limited resources," he says with a shrug, gesturing at the landscape, dotted with boulders and clusters of cacti.

"Isn't it beautiful?" Lane says to Mandy, the two of them looking out at the desert in front of them. They've set up camp beside the river, which froths gently against a shore of red sand, the violet rocks with their gorgeous poisonous algae lining the water.

"It's kind of pretty," Mandy admits. "In a way."

Someone passes around a flask of whiskey, and the women talk amongst themselves, sharing shyly their collective, limited experience with drugs. Gladys has tried marijuana. Allison has some experience with Percocet, but that was mostly for her back. Lane feels a sensation of cautious hope: She and Mandy are getting on with the group. She herself has taken a couple of large swigs from the flask and is feeling warm and happy. She wears a headband with a light attached to the front and feels a bit like God; whoever she turns her attention upon is suddenly cast in a white beam of light. She smiles at her daughter.

"Mom, ow, you're blinding me with that thing." Mandy rubs her eye. "Why didn't you just get a normal flashlight?"

Lane feels the familiar itch of irritation. "This was on *the list*," she says.

Mandy opens her mouth and screams. *An odd reaction*, Lane thinks, before she sees the long black snake that zigs through the circle of women. A few half-hearted screams echo her daughter's. Some of the old ladies scramble onto their tiny camp chairs, barely a foot off the ground. Mandy tries to climb onto hers but it won't hold; she is a solid, muscular girl and the chair is old and baggy, an extra one that Allison offered to Mandy when she realized that everyone else had brought their own. Allison herself sits contentedly on the ground, fiddling with a legitimate-looking pocket knife.

"Mandy—here," Lane says, rising to her feet and holding out her hand to help her daughter scramble onto a medium-sized boulder a few yards away. Mandy clambers onto the rock, crouching there, her knees clutched in her arms, safely out of the snake's way. Relief rushes over Lane, an old motherly impulse. She herself has never feared snakes, though she dislikes bees and certain types of moth.

Lorenzo is standing up, investigating. The snake has gone off in the direction of the riverbank. "Poor little fella," Lorenzo says. "He was terrified."

The women look at each other, perched awkwardly on their flimsy chairs. They laugh in relief.

"Mandy Mayo," Lorenzo says, spotting Lane's daughter alone on her rock. "What are you doing all the way up there?"

Mandy shifts her weight, folding her legs beneath her so that she's sitting more comfortably. She shrugs. "Best seat in the house."

Lane's shoulders slump down in relaxation. Her daughter, for all her brusqueness, has a tendency toward oversensitivity, easily wounded by joking words. *Thank you, Mandy*, she thinks. Mandy is sallying forth. Mandy is not making a scene. Lane feels grateful to her daughter for this kindness.

They go to sleep early, just after the sun sets. When Mandy is snoring in her sleeping bag, Lane clicks on her headlamp to venture out to the makeshift toilet, which Lorenzo has set up down the shore, behind a large boulder, for privacy. As it turns out, the bucket has a toilet seat lid atop it and really isn't so different than a port-a-john. Better, even: Lorenzo has set the whole thing up to face the river, and the view, if you could see it in the dark, is spectacular.

∽○∾

The dawning of sunlight the next day feels to Lane like Christmas morning. She quietly unzips the tent, Mandy still sleeping inside, and joins the women who have begun to congregate around Lorenzo. He has set out blueberry muffins and instant coffee, and heats water in small batches on a battery-operated coil, stirring little packets of non-dairy creamer into it tenderly, with great care.

"Here." He hands Lane her small Styrofoam cup. "It's hot. Be careful."

Mandy emerges from the tent with messy hair and sleep-worn eyes. Lane waves at her. "There's coffee!" she calls, forgetting that her daughter professes not to drink caffeine. But Mandy, perhaps defeated by the events of the day before, tiredly drains a cup of the stuff and thanks Lorenzo.

As soon as they're fed, Lorenzo announces that their hike will begin in ten minutes. They're going two miles further in, to a tiny clearing where the ground becomes rocky and untenable for camping. They'll leave their tents and other gear; they'll be back that night, after the effects have worn off and it's safe to hike again. "Bring your day pack," he says.

Mandy seems docile, content enough to tag along with her mother on this drug-using journey, and Lane tries to swallow the BAD MOTHER lump that has risen in her throat, the one that she used to detect when she got impatient with her daughter, when she scolded her for walking too slowly or speaking too loudly or any of those other natural, childish behaviors that used to annoy Lane so. The annoyance she'd felt upon Mandy's arrival is suddenly gone, replaced with a nervous fear. *Anxiety stomachache*, she used to tell Lonnie it felt like, the feeling that she'd done badly in some unknown way, that consequences would surely descend upon her soon. She decides, firmly, to ignore the feeling: she has two days' vacation time plus $695 invested in enjoying herself.

"Let's go," Lorenzo says, and they line up like ducklings falling in behind their mother.

The hike is beautiful. The morning sun glitters on the river, and even the cacti are splendid in their stark, prickly way. Lane and Mandy lead the group, Lorenzo beside them. A squirrel chatters loudly. "Nature is magnificent," Lane says, reaching a hand out.

"Right, leave those squirrels alone," Lorenzo says. "They bite."

An hour or so later, the trail ends in a small clearing of sand near the shore. "Here we are," Lorenzo says. Lane is surprised to see a weather-worn tent pitched between two boulders, evidence of somebody's campsite.

"Knock knock," Lorenzo calls in the direction of the tent. "Yolandita! We're here."

A dark-haired woman emerges from the tent wearing a caftan painted in reds and golds, hoops dangling from her ears. Lane smiles at her and bows slightly at the waist, wondering who she is—an indigenous person? A drug/spirit guide?—but she greets them in a mild Southern accent. "So good to see y'all. Welcome."

Lorenzo puts his arm around her. "Yolandita's been running our San Pedro sessions since oh-six," he says. "She does a fabulous job."

"Do you *live* down here?" Betty asks. Her face shines with wonderment.

Yolandita laughs. "Lord, no," she says. "I have a condo in Mesa."

"Here's how it'll work," Lorenzo says. "Yolandita has prepared individual servings of cactus extract, twenty-five grams apiece. You'll take it like a shot. Everyone knows what a shot is, yes? Good. You'll feel some mild nausea in the first half-hour or so, but after that you'll start experiencing the most beautiful trip. There's nothing like it, really. It's a very spiritual experience."

"You're very lucky," Yolandita agrees. She gestures. "Walk this way."

Despite the slight oddness of the set-up—Lorenzo hadn't mentioned Yolandita, had he? And what exactly did he mean by *extract?*—Lane feels a pulse of excitement. *This is it.* She and the other women follow Yolandita around the back of her tent, where a weathered picnic table is set up. On the table are several neat rows of little paper cups, lined up like Gatorade ready for thirsty marathoners. "Cactus juice," she says. The women lean in, trying to get a better view.

"What is this?" Lane says. She looks around, at the other women. "I thought we were going to be harvesting the cactus ourselves."

Yolandita and Lorenzo laugh. "Oh, no, dear," Yolandita says. "The San Pedro hardly grows anymore in this part of the world— this stuff's imported from Bolivia."

"It's just as good," Lorenzo says. "Better, even."

Lane feels a rush of disappointment. She looks at the picnic table, at the old women around it like chickens gathering by a feed bucket, and feels the distinct urge to throw a tantrum. She'd wanted to wander off, to find the cactus herself, to pull it up from the earth with her hands. To eat it raw and fresh. As she's grown older, Lane has begun to pride herself on her unflappability, her stalwart adherence to practicality, her lack of vulnerability against the emotional eruptions caused by life's small disappointments. *Who really gets what they want?* she'd thought privately when Mandy had mourned so lengthily and earnestly about Jad. But now, looking at the little cups of green liquid, looking so official, so *processed,* as they sit there in their neat rows, Lane feels the ache of wanting one certain thing so badly: It seems so very little to ask.

"Plus," Yolandita is saying. "The taste of fresh cactus buttons is very, very bad."

"It's foul," Lorenzo agrees.

She gets in line to receive her cactus juice. Maybe, she tells herself, it won't be so bad. Maybe this is the most one can hope for. Mandy floats near her: not in line, exactly, but not so far away, either.

Lorenzo is passing around the little cups to the row of campers. "None for her," Lane says when he gets to them, pointing a thumb at her daughter.

"Oh, no." Yolandita says. "That's not how it works. Everyone partakes." She looks at Lorenzo.

He nods. "Sorry," he says. "No spectators."

Lane glances at Mandy. "Actually," she says, "there was a small mistake. Mandy, see, she didn't know that this was, uh—she didn't know what the trip was actually *for*, ha ha, a bit of a mix-up on both our parts. But she's okay, really. She can read her book over there. Mandy, hon, did you bring your book?"

"It's fine, Mom," Mandy says. "I'll do it."

"Really?" Lane pauses. "Are you sure?"

Mandy nods. "I sort of decided last night."

"Good." Yolandita hands each of them a cup.

Lane feels a pricking gratefulness, sharp and strong as a tetanus shot received before one is prepared. Mandy, who abstains from sugar and only drinks red wine for the revesterol, has been bracing herself to do illegal drugs. Lane feels a small but significant measure of astonished gratitude. Motherhood has not been easy, its difficulties not the ones Lane had expected. Ever since Mandy was a small child Lane has had a sense of unbelonging: Lonnie and Mandy had been closer with each other than they were with her, the two of them often staying up late weekend nights with their heads bent over tiny matchbox cars or watching some documentary in the den that she found tediously boring. Lane hadn't taken to being a mother like she'd expected to. She'd never had a promising career, and so being good at raising her child seemed the most natural path. But even if Mandy had been more interested in the things Lane had to offer, she was no good at baking and disliked arts and crafts, the glittery sludge of them. She had few other ideas; it seemed like arts and crafts were mostly what you did with little girls.

But Mandy is here with her now and she is here with Mandy; there is that. Lane finds her daughter's hand with her own and squeezes it firmly.

"It looks sort of like Mountain Dew," Betty says, looking down into her cup.

"I can assure you it won't taste like it," Lorenzo says.

Yolandita is handing out folded-up paper bags.

"What are these for?" Mandy asks.

"You know, just in case," Yolandita says. She makes a motion of her finger going down her throat. "Of course, you're also welcome to find a private spot by the river somewhere."

Lorenzo raises his little paper cup in the air. "A toast," he says. "To all of you. For coming down here. For opening yourself to new experiences, and to the earth. Don't think too hard. Don't worry about what experience you feel like you should be having. Everyone's different. Just let yourself . . . *be*."

"On the count of three," he says, "swallow the entire contents of your cup. Ready? One, two . . ."

Lane looks at the other women. They raise their cups, toasting one another. "Cheers," Mandy says quietly, and Lane touches her cup to her daughter's.

"Three."

Lane swallows. The taste is vile. *Like drinking the essence of the earth itself*, Mandy will later say. Lane forces the stuff down, alternating swigs from her water bottle with tiny sips of cactus juice. She sees the other women using the same strategy, their faces maintaining expressions of determined happiness, like listening to a bad concert put on by children.

"Oh, my," Gladys says. "This is quite disgusting."

Lane looks over at Mandy, whose cup is empty.

"Are you okay?" she asks.

"Fine," Mandy says, and vomits into her paper bag.

Some amount of time passes; Lane isn't certain how much. She sits near Mandy and the other women, waiting for the cactus to take effect. The part about her not ever having done illegal drugs is only partially true: She'd smoked pot once, when she was twenty-two, just after graduation. She was in Amsterdam with a college friend she has long since fallen out of touch with, and the two of them had nervously sought out and smoked a joint in a dank coffee shop basement, where they sat next to a group of Ukrainian men who were reciting, with great vigor, all of the states of the American East Coast.

She watches Gladys rub Betty's back and feels a hazy kinship toward the group of women, with their pointed elderly knees and their kindness to one another and their enthusiasm for the San Pedro Cactus. And then she feels nausea churn her belly and makes her way to the river to throw up once, and then, a few minutes later, again. She heaves loudly until nothing more comes up but her own thin saliva, vaguely green.

"How are you feeling?" she says to the woman next to her, who turns out to be Allison.

"Pretty good," Allison says. "I think." With great concentration, she is dipping her big toe in and out of the water at the river's edge.

"I don't feel anything," Lane says, looking around, and then a squirrel goes by, leaving lavender squirrel-shaped rings in its wake.

She wanders over to the picnic table. At the edge of her consciousness she notices that Yolandita has laid out a bowl of potato chips. She absently picks up a chip and eats it. *Barbecue*, she thinks. *How nice*. The crunching of the chip between her own teeth sounds immensely loud.

Where is Mandy? It occurs to her that it's been a while since she's seen her daughter; or maybe it's only been a few minutes. Or an hour. It's suddenly impossible to tell. "Mandy," she calls, and then, again, more loudly: *"Mandy!"*

She feels a hand on her shoulder. "She's right over there." Lorenzo points.

Mandy is further down the riverbank, hopping sure-footedly between the slick violet boulders. *Always the athlete*, Lane thinks proudly. As a little girl Mandy had been an excellent runner, fast and slight and darting. Lane had loved watching her get up a head of steam, legs tumbling everywhere. When she got older she'd joined the soccer team, quicker than anyone else on the field, lithe and strong as a colt as she chased down the ball. When she ran like that, she got a look in her eyes like she was lost to the world, a girl in some alternate reality, transcending the soccer field with its patchy grass and chain-link fence. There was something almost spiritual in watching her, the way she cut deftly between defenders without touching them, going by so quickly that it was almost like she'd never been there. In all other elements of life Mandy was curt, gruff, but in athletic competitions she was gracious, almost meek, joking with the other girls, complimenting them on their skills, her vastly greater talent allowing her this kindness. It was as if running set Mandy free of herself.

Lane hadn't thought about that for a long time.

She feels pleasantly drowsy, and closes her eyes. When she opens them, she looks at the purple boulders, which are shrinking and growing very fast, over and over again. She wanders slowly in the direction of the river's edge.

"Mom." At once her daughter is beside her. Mandy's face is wide and smiling and a little bit wavy, like a TV with bad reception. She has pulled her hair back into a ponytail, and she looks young and happy and a tiny bit dazed.

"Look at this." She holds out something that is morphing in size and color too fast for Lane to comprehend, something that might be a rock or a dead fish or a piece of metal from an alien spaceship and then Mandy is pressing it into Lane's palm; it is hers to keep, whatever it is, this offering from her daughter. Perhaps, Lane thinks, the men don't matter so much after all. She feels love for her daughter radiating out of her like the light of the sun. *You are my daughter and I am your mother.* Mandy tilts her head at her and Lane is pretty sure she has actually spoken these words out loud and then Mandy is off again, leaping between rocks, a rainbow of color following her, a spinning vortex of reds and blues and yellows.

"Men," Lane says out loud. "Who needs them?"

"I'm not a lesbian," Allison says.

"Oh," Lane says. "I'm not, either."

She holds her treasure tight in her hand and she looks at her daughter, and it's only for a second but she sees a girl running down a field of grass, moving too fast for safety; a girl with her whole life ahead of her: a girl young and bright and full of promise.

The Year of Perfect Happiness

*A year of perfect happiness, just the sound of it, a single year
locked away from the years before it and the years after it,
happiness unburdened by nostalgia, perfect. . . .*

—*Kevin Moffett, "The Volunteer's Friend"*

January

Winter in the city depresses Davis, the grimy slushiness of it,
the graduated shades of gray that make up the street, the sky, the
dirty snow banks. It is as if the gray trumps all else, Technicolor
dragged through dishwater, drained of its brilliance. He can feel it
seeping into him, the slow trickle getting into his brain, freezing
him like an icicle.

"I'm moving," he tells Angie over dinner—Angie, who
is more than a roommate and less than a girlfriend—and she
wrinkles her nose.

"No, you aren't," she says and stabs at her food with her fork.
He's prepared tofu *parmigiana* for dinner; he and Angie have
worked together to perfect his method of cooking tofu, pressing
it before dry-frying it and then dipping in egg and breadcrumbs
and sautéing. Tomato sauce and mozzarella are cooked on top,
browned under the broiler.

"Yes, I am," he says, watching her over his wine, sipping without taking his eyes off her. "To Arizona. I'll keep paying my half of the rent until the lease is up."

For Davis, happiness is traveling. Or, more precisely, relocating—the newness, the freshness of things, the uncontaminated goodness of a place where one has not lived and had time to become aware of its ugliness, its scrapes and nicks, the ghosts of things gone wrong while you lived there. He has a reason for moving, a nascent curl of a plan, an idea that occurred to him when his girlfriend before Angie, Chloe, broke things off with him: He wants to locate a year of perfect happiness in his life, just one year, a year that he will be able to look back on and remember as the twelve months during which *he was happy*. Searching his memory, he can isolate weeks of happiness in his life, a month, even, here or there, but not a year—not even close—and this seems to him a great shame.

The moving is a part of this plan. He will go from each place when this happiness begins to sour, to curl at the edges, become tainted. Before this ugliness grows, he will move on and begin anew, maintaining his happiness; this is his plan. New York he is tired of. It is time to go.

"I have a business idea," he is telling Angie. "It's called ForageFarm. It's going to be a mix between a co-op and an assisted gardening program. Because people want to eat locally, you know, grow their own food? Eat things without GMOs and pesticides. But they don't know how to go about it. That's where I come in." He cracks his knuckles with satisfaction. "I'll set up a system of going around and helping people plant gardens in their own yards and tending these gardens, harvesting them, whatever else. But that's not all—I'll set up a sharing system among neighbors, so, say, if you've got extra tomatoes and you want some fresh sage or chives or something you don't grow, you can make a trade. I'm planning a website, the works." This is his official excuse for quitting his job at H&R Block and moving about as he pleases, though he doesn't tell Angie this. Besides, engaging his entrepreneurial spirit is an idea that appeals to him, a move he sees as a cornerstone of locating this newly established happiness (because isn't that what happiness is, anyway: doing something you're good at and knowing that you're helping people at the same time?)

"Why don't you do it here?" she asks. "I could help you. I could make the flyers or help you with your website. Create a logo for you. Smiling carrots and broccoli, or whatever."

This stops him momentarily—Angie is a graphic designer; her skills would surely come in handy—but he shakes his head.

"No," he says firmly, and then, softer: "Sorry, Ang, this is something I have to do."

"Just because you grow basil in the window box doesn't mean you know how to plant a garden," she says bitterly. "Besides, ForageFarm is a stupid name. It doesn't even mean the right thing." That's Angie: sweet, suppliant one moment, stormy the next, like a child. He's going to miss her.

"I don't think you'll really go," she says, but she pouts in a way that lets him know she knows he is serious, and she won't look at him when he offers to do the dishes, this a small and inadequate peace offering for the fact that he is leaving her.

March

He likes how different Phoenix is from New York, the expanse of the surrounding desert so luxurious, so unreal after his five years in Midtown. He likes the dramatic swell of the land, likes the huge, looming saguaros, the prickly pear cactuses, the Joshua trees. People who live in the city here have yards, front lawns landscaped with rocks of varying sizes—pebbles to boulders—and with carefully placed Southwestern artifacts: an old wooden wagon wheel, a dreamcatcher adorned with colorful feathers, an outdoor stove made of adobe. There is hardly a blade of grass to be seen. It is almost like living in an alternate universe, except that the people here are much the same as the people in New York, if less stylishly dressed.

He sets up a life for himself that pleases him greatly, doing the things he has observed in others he admires—shopping regularly at the farmers market, hiking, reading books, real books. (He begins with the Russian masters, planning to move next to the Victorians.) He trains for his first half-marathon, watches the loose folds of his belly get firm, his skinny-guy flabbiness disappear. He looks in on himself as he imagines a third-person observer might and is pleased with what he sees—and isn't that happiness, anyway, establishing a version of yourself that you like and then maintaining that self, doing things that make you proud?

He gets an assistant manager job at a co-op, though he doesn't need it: Davis's mom is a real estate agent, dealing in the multi-million-dollar properties of the Florida coastline. Before he retired, his dad was a genetic scientist, had several patents to his name that Davis understood to be significant—something about protein sequences. His parents have always been generous, rarely giving him cash without occasion but writing big checks for important events: his college graduation, his move to New York, plus whatever birthdays his mother found especially important. (His thirtieth had been the latest, a couple of years ago—there was a check for ten grand folded into a card that said HAPPY BIRTHDAY on the outside and THIRTY IS JUST EIGHTEEN WITH TWELVE YEARS OF EXPERIENCE on the inside.) He's never had a lot of extra cash, but always enough to stay afloat. Plus, his parents had given him a sleek, silver new BMW X5 after college, which he sold when he got to New York, priding himself on only using public transportation, though he's bought a '94 Jetta, for use in Phoenix and for traveling.

He tells himself that he will begin laying the groundwork for ForageFarm as soon as he gets settled; the truth is, he's nervous. Angie was right—he actually knows very little about gardening, and in choosing Arizona for its perpetual heat, for the fact that he could get started right away with the project, he had failed to consider just how drastic an impact the climate might have on his plants. He is afraid. He checks out books from the library, making charts of planting dates, taking notes about soil mixing and hydrogels, and tells himself he will begin his gardening foray soon—but not now. Later, maybe when he arrives at his next destination.

More importantly, he has worked out the ground rules for his year of perfect happiness in his head: flashes of malice, of inconvenience—a rude cashier at the market, a quarrel with his father during a Sunday phone call, a long run postponed by bad weather—these don't count. It is the maintenance of a day-to-day happiness that matters, the ability for the good to overtake the bad on a nightly basis, the ability to answer in the affirmative to the question Am I Happy? But a dulling, dreary, dissatisfaction, a lingering discontent—this is unhappiness; this ruins it; he must make a change before this takes hold of him.

He sends Angie a postcard with the words IT'S A DRY HEAT captioned below a picture of a skeleton in a hat and spurs slumped against a cactus. He finds this very funny: *Ha ha ha!* He writes on the back. *Love, Davis.*

It is a good start.

May

In the spring there is Amanda, a tall and glamorous redhead, a mid-level executive at a downtown firm specializing in grassroots advertising. She wears two-piece suits of muted colors to work and takes no greater pleasure than having lunch with her friends from work, eating sushi or bagel sandwiches with similarly well-dressed women also in suits of muted colors, shades of charcoal and bone, with tasteful and understated jewelry. She invited Davis once to meet up with the bunch of them, and it amused him to watch them take small, careful bites, make polite little jokes, chat about their coworkers and boss. Amanda is athletic in a quiet, unshowy way, likes to hike and rock-climb; she takes him to the rock gym with her and makes encouraging little comments to him as the climbing instructor, a kid with a mohawk and lean, ropy muscles in his arms, guides him up the beginners' wall.

Dating her both invigorates and reinforces the version of himself that he likes. They make an intelligent, handsome, liberal couple. They bring their own canvas bags to the grocery store and picnic regularly on Sundays with a crusty loaf of bread, some pesto and the *Times*. They go to gourmet beer tastings and community playhouse productions. The sex is good, if not thrilling—she is put-together and glamorous even in bed, with expensive lingerie and a nightstand full of the necessary goodies: condoms and lube and toys set in a neat row in the drawer. He feels sure that her friends like him, and this pleases him because isn't that all happiness is anyway, immersing yourself in a community of thoughtful and intelligent people?

Soon, though, he discovers an underside to Amanda's personality, the way you do when you spend your nights and mornings and weekends with a person. Amanda's underside is hard, gritty, sharpened. She becomes increasingly competitive, at first only in athletics, pushing him to accompany her on advanced hikes, and then eventually in everything, like whose childhood was more fraught or who lost more weight on the glycemic index diet that they've decided to try and who has a more neutralized carbon footprint, blah, blah, *blah*. She gets angry when he tells her how many women he's slept with, even though she asked; she acts like he is hiding things from her. Soon it becomes clear to Davis that there is a meticulousness embedded in her DNA that extends to him, too: She gets angry when he forgets that it's his night to make dinner and comes home at nine after catching a movie by himself.

"Why didn't you just eat without me?" he asks after he's gotten it out of her why she's pissed.

Her face goes crimson at the suggestion. "I thought it would've been rude, Davis," she says. "To break our agreement. To renege on an established plan."

He has to stop himself from smiling. This is one of the things he loves about her, despite her recent pissiness—this formal way of addressing him in the same tone of voice that she might use to give a PowerPoint at work. "I'm sorry," he says. "Really, I am. I'll go pick something up. Right now. I'll go down and get some veggie subs. Hey. Okay?" He nods at her until she tilts her head up in acknowledgement: "Okay."

Later, working on the bottle of Shiraz they'd had with dinner, she asks why he never bought a condo when he was living in New York.

He shrugs. "Everything's so expensive. I couldn't've gotten anything good."

"But did you ever think about it? Did you even try?" She herself owns an impeccable downtown condo, a soft-loft with custom shoe racks in the closet and meticulously placed décor which creates a pretty nice aesthetic effect—her place looks fantastic, Davis has to admit, all sleek lines and dark wood—but some of which seems to him less than functional, more trouble than it's worth. Every time he stays over, she removes decorative pillows from the bed before they go to sleep or have sex, stacking them in a neat pile and placing them in the armoire. It's kind of a buzz kill.

He pours more wine; she tilts her glass so he can refill it. "I don't know," he says. "I guess not." He clears his throat. "You know,

I've been thinking a lot about this ForageFarm thing. Remember, the thing I told you about? I'm thinking I really might try to start things up. Get the proverbial wheels turning."

"I looked it up," she says, ignoring him. "For what you pay monthly here plus the amount you could have put toward a down payment, you could have gotten a place with almost the same square footage that you have now. In a decent neighborhood, too."

This pisses him off. "I didn't want to, okay? I didn't know how long I'd be in New York. I would've had to sell when I moved—I could've lost money."

She puts up her hands, one still holding her wine glass. "Davis, I was just asking."

"I feel like you're starting to resent me."

She considers this. "I don't resent you," she says after a moment. "I guess I just wish I had the money to pay two rents while I fucked around for a year."

July

He goes to see his parents in Florida, swallowing the feeling that by going home he is cheating a bit. The truth is he fled Arizona quickly, before he expected to, in order to preserve the integrity of his year of happiness. This is how he's begun to think of it—a year of happiness, dropping the "perfect" because to be *perfectly happy*, that's impossible, really, he knows that now, but to be *happy*—is achievable. (And isn't it more reasonable, he asks himself, to hope that you may become realistically satisfied with your life rather than ecstatic with it?) He and Amanda had continued to fight, arguing in a quiet, sarcastic way, bored with one another: the worst kind of way to fight, and with no sex afterward.

His parents live in Fort Myers, in a sprawling, Spanish-style split-level sixty yards from the beach. The last time he was here, he'd been three years out of college, had just moved into his first place in Manhattan and was bursting to prove the sophistication and intelligence he'd acquired by living in the city.

On the plane, he'd read an article in the *Times* about how manicured lawns were really nothing more than an antiquated status symbol; the article's author argued that people should quit spending their time and their (limited!) resources attempting to make their yards look like green carpet, and this was, of course, the argument that Davis had parroted to his parents on the ride home from the airport—to his dad, especially, who took particular pride in his exceptionally well-groomed lawn, which was approximately as large as a football field.

"It might be a status symbol," his dad said, "but I don't want my lawn filled with a bunch of weeds. Who does?"

"That's the point, Dad," Davis said, trying to keep his voice from rising to a high, excited pitch. "That's exactly the point. People think of naturally occurring plants as weeds, but it's all just a matter of taxonomy. Who decides what's a weed and what's not, after all? It's just—"

His dad held up a hand to stop him. "Don't say 'it's just semantics,'" he said, which was in fact what Davis was going to say, one of his new favorite phrases, picked up from a friend. "Because it's *not*."

At dinner Davis had announced, with gusto, that he had become a vegetarian—he was trying to transition to vegan, actually, hopefully by the end of the month—and he had given what he'd thought to be a very informed and inspirational speech about collective social and moral imperatives as they related to food consumption. He'd been so pleased with himself that it was almost possible to ignore the look on his mother's face as she'd stood, serving fork poised, over the beef daube Provençal.

But there is none of this ugliness now. His mother made a vegetable lasagna for dinner on the night of his arrival, but in the morning forgets and offers him a bacon-and-egg biscuit so earnestly that he accepts it and eats it sitting on a stool at the kitchen counter, facing his mother.

"This is good," he says, and he isn't lying—it is.

"Thanks, baby," his mom says. She is standing at the sink, scrubbing fiercely at the baked-on crud from the biscuit pan. She is dressed in a bright red pants suit—she's about to leave for an open house—and watching her, Davis thinks her appearance is exactly the cliché of a real estate agent. When she'd gotten her license and started showing homes, she'd begun to dress in the way she assumed real estate agents were meant to dress, all heels and power suits and tight, slicked-back hairstyles that make her forehead too large for her petite face, her eyebrows now emphasized, giving her a perpetually surprised expression, as if someone has just asked her a question she doesn't know the answer to.

"What do you have planned for today, Davey?" she says, putting the pan in the dish drainer and wiping her hands.

He shrugs. The truth is that he'd looked forward to a lazy day, a day of lounging and swimming at his parents' pool and later settling in front of their massive television. He'd deprived himself of cable in New York and Arizona and is looking forward to a few hours of aimless channel-surfing, of watching whatever is on HBO or even the network channels. Idiotic sitcoms or reality programs, anything, really, will do. "Haven't decided yet," he says, rising to refill his mug. "I might go out to the trails later, if Dad doesn't mind me using his bike."

"Why don't you come to the open house?"

He winces. "I don't know, Mom, I'm not good at schmoozing people."

She rolls her eyes. "You'd hardly be there to schmooze, Davey." She gestures at his clothes, a grubby hoodie and a pair of black jeans faded to gray, and he has the distinct feeling of being returned to his teenage self, a feeling he has often when he comes home. "You'll be there for me. In case nobody shows up—so I won't be bored. Or embarrassed."

"Or," Davis says, "I can put on my suit and pretend like I'm some hot-shit lawyer coming to make an offer on the place. You know, to motivate the other prospective buyers."

"If you're going to do that, you're not coming."

"Okay," he says, and grins, stirring milk into his coffee, a habit that has always annoyed him—his inability to drink it black. "Okay, I'll go."

At the open house, he sees immediately that she was lying— if not lying, then at least deceiving him in suggesting that maybe no one would show. A crowd of at least fifteen streams into the house when they open the doors at noon, after the two of them have set out a tray of flatbread and Brie, after he has helped his mother vacuum the oak floors and polish the already pristine bathroom and kitchen fixtures. The house is stunning, a water-front property not unlike his parents' own home, decorated in an ocean motif so consistent as to appear calculated, which Davis snorted at upon their arrival but which creates an effect he has to admit is beautiful: elegant floor vases filled with dried cattails, white wood furniture set against blue-gray walls, an art wall in the great room with nine square-framed black-and-white photographs of the shore hung symmetrically in rows of three, forming one larger square.

He has put on a dress shirt and tie at his mother's request. He's never been good at tying a tie, "a sign that I really wasn't cut out for corporate America," he sometimes jokes, and he tugs on the big, gnarly knot at his neck as he walks around by himself, admiring the house but really looking more at the cur-rent owners' possessions than at the crown molding and quartz countertops that everyone downstairs is going so nuts over. He is inside the gargantuan master-bedroom closet, marveling over rows and rows of ladies' blouses and blazers and evening gowns, each hanger equidistant from the next, when a woman's voice startles him.

"The kitchen and living room I bought, but this can't be real. Right?"

"I'm sorry?"

She is about his height and tan, really tan, her skin darkened to a deep nut brown, her white-blond hair giving way to a half-inch of dark roots at her scalp. Her shoulders and décolletage are spotted with the permanent freckles that a person gets from spending many hours of many days in the sun. Davis thinks if he got closer, she might smell like saltwater, or seaweed. She gestures at the immaculate closet. "This. Does anybody actually keep their clothes this way? Do the Realtors demand that people dry-clean all their clothes and then organize them by color? Or are these fake clothes, and the owners have their real things stuffed into suitcases in a motel?" She laughs, a big, unself-conscious laugh, and Davis can nearly see down her throat.

"I don't know," he says thoughtfully. It's true—the house is not only impeccably clean, but looks hardly lived in—but the evidence is here, shoes and shirts and scarves. "I'd have to ask my mother," he says.

"Your mother?"

Davis's cheeks flush hot. "She's the Realtor."

"Ahh, so you're—"

"Here with her, yeah. No, I'm definitely not a potential buyer." He looks her over, and it occurs to him that she isn't either. Her clothes aren't of the same quality as those of the women downstairs, and there is something about the shade of her lipstick—too bright, too harshly applied. "Are you?" he asks bluntly.

"Is that so hard to believe?"

"I don't know, I—"

She waves a hand. "It's all right," she says. "You caught me. There's no way I could ever afford a place like this. Just don't tell your mom." She sticks out a hand, a tanned paw with long, acrylic fingernails. No ring on either hand. "I'm Lynn," she says.

September

They begin seeing one another regularly, and everyone is happy with this arrangement: Lynn, who claims to like to cook for more than herself and her cat; Davis, who finds her surprisingly good company, honest and funny and a good judge of people, despite the alarming fingernails; Davis's parents, who are relieved to have him out of the house four or five nights a week. He and Lynn cook dinner together or pick up take-out on the nights she doesn't have to work at the hospital where she is a pediatric nurse. They go to movies and to the mall, where she likes to go into the candy store and buy jelly beans in bulk, eating them slowly as they walk in and out of department stores, where she fingers items but never buys them, brushing her hands over entire racks of clothing Davis suspects she would never have occasion to wear: beaded evening gowns, expensive silk scarves, tailored dress shirts.

She is an excellent cook, better than he, for all his efforts with classes and cookbooks and potted herbs in window boxes; Lynn has a natural flair for creating dishes, for blending flavors and textures. He hasn't told her about ForageFarm—*yet*, he tells himself, trying to believe he will definitely tell her when he gets things off the ground, but the guilt of it sits in his belly like a thing undone.

He is eating meat again since the bacon and egg biscuit, which is good because Lynn likes grilling out, steak kabobs and beer burgers or else hearty pasta dishes with lots of chicken or fish, or spaghetti with huge, spicy meatballs.

"What's the point?" she says, genuinely confused, when he asks why she never prepares meatless entrees. She is making a dish she calls "beer can chicken," and he watches as she rams a can of Miller Lite into the cavity of the chicken's ass, grunting at the effort.

"What are you doing?"

She has situated the beer can to her liking and is trussing the legs with string. "What?"

"Are you going to leave it there like that? Couldn't you just pour some beer over the skin?"

When she turns to face him, she has a huge smile on her face. "The chicken can't feel it, you know—it's *dead*," she says. "I never pegged you to be so squeamish."

He opens his mouth to say something and then closes it again, realizing that he has come to a point where it would be foolish tell Lynn he used to practice some semblance of vegetarianism. He feels far and distant from this Davis who used to eschew meat, has had to admit even to himself that the discrepancy between the Davis he wants to be and the Davis he is, who lives in Florida with no job and is sleeping with a woman who hasn't voted, *ever*, is giving him a bit of a headache, but that when he can manage to ignore it everything feels pretty good. He feels more like himself than he has in years, as if he had been covered in a layer of ice that has now cracked and fallen away. He reminds himself quite often that this is what he loves about Lynn: If nothing else, she is herself.

He hadn't planned to stay in Florida, would have considered it a failure to exist in the place of his upbringing, but he thinks of this with increasingly less frequency as the days pass. Lynn is off on Saturdays, and they spend most of these days at the pool: It's still hot in September, the sunlight reflecting in a white blaze off the water, and sometimes as Davis lies on his pool chair, hands folded behind his head, feet crossed at the ankles, with Lynn napping in the chair next to him, he thinks: Maybe this is it. Maybe this is the happiness; if I maintain this for one year *I will be happy*. Because after all, isn't this what happiness is: being with another person who not only allows you to be yourself but who requires it?

"Can I ask you something?" he says one day. It is a Saturday, and they have just arrived at the pool. Lynn is shaking out a towel before spreading it over one of the white plastic lounge chairs. She turns to him, her hand shielding her eyes. "Yeah. What's up?"

"Why were you at that open house? You said you weren't looking to buy."

She goes back to shaking the towel, and he covers his face to avoid getting hit by the little bits of grass and rock that fly from it. "I don't know," she says after a moment, giving the towel a final, vigorous shake and then spreading it over the chair and smoothing it with her hands. "I guess it's something about—" she hesitates. "I guess there's something about seeing beautiful things that I love. It's hard to explain, but when I found out about the open house, I felt drawn to go—I felt like even if I'll never be able to afford so much as a toilet in a house like that, I shouldn't be deprived of seeing the beauty of it; like that shouldn't be something that's reserved for only rich people." She has positioned herself atop the pool chair, but now, lying on her side, she props herself on one elbow so that she is facing him. "Does that make sense?"

"Don't kid yourself," he jokes, "you were there for the free food."

She doesn't laugh. "I don't do it anymore," she says, "but I have this mink stole that my grandmother gave me, and I know it's totally politically incorrect and everything, but the thing is *beautiful*; it's the softest thing you ever touched, and I used to put it on and go out to eat by myself at Richie's. It wasn't that I was trying to pick up guys, nothing like that. I just liked to pretend that I was rich and gorgeous, one of these 1920s beauties—you know, the women in the movies with their hair curled onto their faces and red lipstick—and I'd order the most expensive thing on the menu." She smiles ruefully at him. "It's stupid, I know. I've never told anyone that before. I guess it's like my little secret, or something."

Davis feels an uneasiness begin to gnaw his belly, which he tells himself isn't because Richie's isn't a nice restaurant but Lynn thinks it is—these things have never before bothered him about Lynn, so why should they bother him now?—but he can't stop imagining Lynn getting into her car by herself and driving downtown, wearing a too-short skirt and a top four or five years out of style and accessories all over the place, plastic hoop earrings and bangles up to her elbows—she always wears too much cheap jewelry—and the thought of it disgusts him because he's always thought of Lynn as so authentic, so herself—nothing like this new version she's now placed before him. She is looking at him expectantly, waiting, having offered up this piece of herself, wanting a response that at once he knows he can't give her.

"I didn't know you liked Richie's," he says casually. "We should go sometime. I heard they have killer ribs."

October

Davis hadn't actually had any real intention of going to eat at Richie's. The whole idea of it made him nervous: the possibility of Lynn in mink and of him being forced into some supporting role in the spectacle of it. But here they are, he having let himself be talked into it, and he makes himself smile at her as they slide into their booth because in all honesty he's begun to acquire a sort of distaste for Lynn, and it is a slippery feeling, one that slides around in him, going away for days at a time only to resurface unexpectedly, a feeling that he is trying to ignore, wants to ignore. It is why he was afraid of coming to Richie's, afraid of the idea of so baldly facing the fact of Lynn, afraid that perhaps it would facilitate the crumbling of some façade held precariously in place. But it's not a bad place to eat, if you don't mind the kitschy décor, the giant fishing nets nailed to the walls, the big canoe hanging from the ceiling, the wooden DO NOT FEED

THE ALLIGATORS sign nailed over the entrance. The waiters, mostly college kids from FGCU, wear bright Hawaiian shirts and black slacks and sneakers. The food, mostly fried, smells good: He watches a plate of fajitas go by, sizzling and popping, and then an order of fried shrimp, served in a little tin bucket surrounded ceremoniously by lettuce leaves.

Lynn is indeed wearing her grandmother's stole, a heavy, brown, literal thing; Davis is grateful that the mink's taxidermied face isn't staring at him from the end of it. There's something disturbing about the whole idea of it, eating the body parts of one animal while wearing another. She is stroking it absently, her hand going over it in the same motion that a person might use to pet a cat, and Davis has to look away.

"It's not the same wearing this thing when you're here," she is saying. "It's like what it represented is gone—the possibility is gone, or something like that. Does that make sense?"

"Maybe the fur is getting to your brain."

She frowns. "What does that mean?"

Davis shrugs, flipping a menu page. "I don't know. Nothing. Sorry."

"I'm getting the ribeye," she announces a moment later. "And some cole slaw. What are you getting?"

"Hmm?"

She snaps her fingers in front of his face. "Earth to Davis. Hello. I'm asking you what you're going to get to eat. For dinner."

"Oh," he says. "Sorry. Umm, the fish and chips, I think." He drums his fingers on the tabletop. "So," he says. "Listen. There's something I want to tell you. It's something I've been thinking about a lot over the past year, and, well, it's—" She is looking at him, and he becomes flustered. "I'm trying to figure out how to be—how to be *happy*," he says quickly, letting go of the eloquent little speech he'd been planning, a speech that would have demonstrated his plan for happiness and its accompanying savvy, instead launching into a description of his plan for ForageFarm, that thing he'd saved, in the back of his mind, still untainted and full of hope, like an unopened package. "There's this thing I've been thinking about doing. It's kind of a business venture. It's called ForageFarm, and what it is is an assisted gardening program, meaning that I'll help people plant their own gardens with organic vegetables and herbs, things like that. If you think about it, in a way, it's one of the nobler things a person can do. It's this way of getting at happiness. Not that I would go around calling myself noble. That would be extremely pompous."

A giggle blossoms from Lynn's mouth. "Come on, Davis," she says. "Gardening? Happiness? *Noble?* Don't tell me now that you've been full of it this whole time and I'm only now catching on." She laughs again, her mouth opening wide, and he actually sees her uvula vibrate a bit. "Plus, you killed all my cilantro, remember?"

Davis frowns. "Yeah, I remember," he says. "I wouldn't be doing the actual gardening, for the most part. I'm more in charge of the conceptual stuff."

"So people would be paying you to tell them to do the work themselves?"

This pisses him off. "What would you do?" he says sourly. "What, exactly, would you do—that would make it so you could be happy?"

"What's wrong with what we're doing right now?"

"Forget it," he says after a moment. "You're right. It's probably just a pipe dream." He picks at a piece of crud that has hardened onto his fork.

"Davis, I'm just giving you a hard time. Of course you can do it. I'll help you, if you want. I've got some experience growing things, as you know." She clicks her nails on the table, and he cringes at the acrylic clatter of them, feeling a surge of dislike for her course through him, and when he looks up at her everything is illuminated: her thick lips that turn down slightly at the corners, her eyes, just a bit too close together—he'd never noticed this—and the makeup that creases in her wrinkles, little beige-colored rivers by the corners of her eyes and mouth. He feels something darken inside him, becoming acerbic, sharp, like a shot of whiskey.

"I don't know," he says cruelly. "I'm beginning to wonder if this thing between us has run its course."

"Davis—"

"You knew this would happen eventually," he says, cutting her off. "Didn't you?"

Their rum runners arrive, big plastic souvenir cups with swizzle sticks of translucent green plastic with little alligator heads on the ends of them. Davis drags his violently through the liquid, which is amber and murky and reminds him of a swamp.

December

It's going to be a green Christmas; it always is in South Florida, temperatures hovering around eighty-five, the air warm and damp and dense as a sponge. Davis wipes his forehead with the back of his hand, and it comes away slick, like it might be after running five or six miles, even though it's seven at night and he's been outside for under twenty minutes, hanging a single string of lights on the front edge of his roof. He is, as a rule, opposed to Christmas decorations, hates the grotesque, inflatable Santas and elves and reindeer that are popular among his neighbors this year, but two days before Christmas he suddenly didn't want to have the only house on the street that remained dark and went to the Wal-Mart for the first time in nearly five years and scoured the holiday decorations. Little remained. What was there was picked over, and he ended up with a string of blue lights about four feet shorter than the length of his roof, which he hadn't realized until he had it almost all the way tacked up, where it gives the impression of a thing going a certain distance before simply giving up.

He's lived here for approaching six weeks: Not having the will of mind nor the strength of heart to make another cross-country trip, he moved to the southeast side of town, ten minutes from his parents, to a rented duplex in a neighborhood that more rightly represents his station in life, what he's earned, what he's worked for—which isn't much. "You know you're welcome to stay here, Davey," his mother had said, but he couldn't bear to stay in their house another day; the Calypso swimming pool and the marble countertops reminded him viscerally and daily of who he was: a thirty-something man who'd quit a steady if uninteresting job, a man who was part of a generation full of opinions and short on cash, who thought themselves deserving of things in life and who were, generally speaking, downwardly mobile and ill-accomplished.

He shares the two-story duplex with a woman named Ellie, a wide-hipped, blonde single mother of two young children, who has given these children a set of drums as an early Christmas gift. Even though Davis has, in the last three weeks, begun experiencing throbbing headaches, his head pounding to the beat of the beating, he doesn't mind, not really, because isn't this all that happiness is, anyway: knowing that you're alive, that you exist, that you are a human who is present in the world, a human who is alive, not dead, capable of responding to stimuli, to sights, sounds, smells?

He isn't seeing Lynn anymore. Quite accidentally, she revealed something bad and wrong about himself, something malignant that he couldn't turn away from in her presence, and he didn't call her again. He has tried to push the whole thing out of his mind, has tried very hard not to ask himself whether a person can be happy in the present when he has acted cruelly in the past, but there is a swelling of unpleasantness that stays at the back of his throat and in his sinuses, like a cold. Lynn didn't call him, a fact that nearly made him reconsider, but then he didn't.

Nor has he made any progress in the creation of ForageFarm, though he has planted a tomato plant in his backyard, a timid, green vine that he tends to gently, sprinkling it with water from a mason jar and pressing fertilizing pellets into the ground, praying that it will make it through the winter; he has been told that this is sometimes possible in South Florida. Ellie sometimes calls to him from her kitchen window as he fusses with his tomato plant, always asking the same thing: "Howsa green thumb?" and he yells something back in response or gives her a thumbs-up, feeling mildly pleased but not overly so, as if her attention to him is a rerun of a TV show he's already seen—not objectionable but not particularly interesting.

Ellie works as day manager at a casual dining burger joint and has on three separate occasions asked Davis to babysit her children while she goes to work, but Davis admires this in her, really he does! Because even though she arrives in his doorway smelling like oil from the Fry-O-Lator and sometimes is thirty or even forty-five minutes late getting back, it's not unpleasant to interact with her, just as he imagines it might be not unpleasant to have her knock quietly on his door after her children are asleep or perhaps just slip in using a key left under the doormat, crawl into a bed he'd already be in, slip a hand between his legs, press herself against him, because isn't this all that happiness is, anyway, failing love or success or intellectual rigor: a warm, living body lying next to yours?

A neighbor, Hank, passes by, and Davis raises his beer in greeting. Hank is his favorite neighbor, a retired army lieutenant who has, in the last two weeks, helped Davis change a flat on his car and unclogged the garbage disposal in Davis's kitchen sink. He watches Hank make his way toward him, his gait halting from some shrapnel he took in the leg at the end of his eighteen months in Vietnam. Davis often has the feeling, speaking to Hank, that they belong to two different species: Hank has fought in a war, fathered children, voted for Eisenhower. Sometimes, blending a smoothie or struggling to assemble his new IKEA sideboard, Davis has the urge to close his blinds. Once, standing on Hank's doorstep to hand over a piece of misdelivered mail, he'd glimpsed the inside of Hank's home, which was furnished with large oriental area rugs and old, expensive-looking pieces of mahogany furniture that had clearly weathered decades of use. Davis's own possessions utterly lack this permanence. His dresser, also from IKEA, is made of painted particle board; he is hoping it will last until he has the money and the inclination to buy one made of actual wood. (As he assembled the dresser, he'd thought dryly what a sad little goal this was, to own furniture made of what it appeared to be made of.)

"Davis, hello," Hank calls now from the edge of Davis's lawn. "Need a hand?"

Davis hops down from the second step of the ladder, borrowed from Hank, and crosses the lawn to meet his neighbor, extending a hand. Hank shakes it firmly. He nods up at Davis's lights. "They look good. How'd you get them so straight?"

A small knob of pride rises in Davis's throat before going quickly away when he glances up at the lights and is reminded of their literal shortcomings; Hank is a kind man. Davis points at the staple gun sitting on the top of the ladder. "I staple between each light," he says. "It keeps them even. My dad always did that. He couldn't stand it when the lights were droopy or uneven."

Hank cocks his head up toward the lights. "Not a bad idea," he says. "I might try that next Christmas. I think it's a bit late for this year." He gestures at his own lights, two houses down, the lines of them straight as rulers and the appropriate length for the roof. "You getting together with your folks later?"

Davis nods. "I'll probably go over tomorrow or the next day."

Hank stands with his hands in his pockets, rocking slightly back and forth. "Carol and I are grilling steaks tonight," he says, nodding toward his house. "If you want to join us. It's just the two of us—we'd be happy for some company."

This is the third invitation Hank has extended to Davis—he has never accepted—and it occurs to him that Hank feels sorry for him, or perhaps it is just that Hank is a good man, much different than himself, who has things that take time and effort to attain and which have never occurred to Davis to want, like mature fruit trees and a sense of neighborly gentility.

"Let me think about that, Hank," Davis says. "I'll finish up these lights and let you know. I've got your number."

"Okay, Davis. We hope to see you." Hank shakes his hand again—Davis is always struck by the formality of this gesture— and watches Hank cross the lawn and join his wife on their front porch.

Ellie's old Honda rounds the corner, rattling to a stop in the driveway, and Davis steps back to give her room to swing the door open. "No kids tonight?"

"Their dad has them a day early this weekend. That way I get them for Christmas." She pulls a grease-soaked paper bag from the passenger's seat. "Have you had dinner? We closed early. Some of the food was still on the line."

He hasn't. "No," he says, and looks at the bag, the bottom of it dark brown and wet-looking. "No, I haven't."

"Well," she says, pulling out a fry and folding the whole thing into her mouth at once, "you're welcome to it. There's plenty."

"Thanks, Ellie."

"No problem." She waves a fry in the air. "Oh! Look—carolers!" She points her fry down the street. "Look!"

Dusk is turning to dark, but he can still see a troupe of carolers approaching at the end of his street, young people, kids, really, teenagers, with a few adults alongside. He smiles obligingly at Ellie. Caroling, in his opinion, is an idea more nostalgic and romantic in theory than in practice, for he never knows quite what to do when the carolers appear and has in the past stayed inside and turned off all his lights before they reached his house.

"Stay here," Ellie says. "I'm going to go get the video camera."

He stays, standing in his front yard, beer in hand, watching the blur of carolers approach, their voices becoming clear and loud as they move closer, and then he realizes that Ellie is back, notices that she is standing very close to him, that her hand has somehow made its way into his without him noticing. This doesn't bother him; in fact it seems about right, her doing this as he might have guessed she would, and as she squeezes his hand, no chills travel up his arm; there are no goose bumps, no belly-dropping sensation. He squeezes back, daring to meet her eyes, but slyly, her hand and his too now slick with grease, and he knows he won't accept Hank's invitation, that after the carolers pass by he and Ellie will go into her house and eat cold hamburgers and fries and that he is an adult and this is his choice. There are worse things that exist in the world, and he is not doing these things; and *this*, he tells himself firmly, *this is happiness*. Momentarily he wonders if there might be a woman in San Antonio or Chicago who is a little like Ellie or maybe not like her at all, and after he turns to smile at her he watches with a wary eye as the mass of people and singing that is the carolers comes closer, a ball of light and sound that is bright but tenuous, diaphanous, as he waits for them to arrive at the front of his lawn, to sing for him.

31901055883500

CPSIA information can be obtained at www.ICGtesting.com
Printed in the USA
LVOW11s0824260914

406016LV00002B/3/P